ST. FINBAR'S CROSS

Dr Claudia Taylor's overbearing mother regards her daughter's general practitioner work as a poor second to 'real medicine'. In order to get out of Manchester as quickly as possible, Claudia takes up a locum position in a Devon village surgery, intending to prove her mother wrong by moving on to a more exciting post overseas once her time there is up. But when mutual attraction flares between Claudia and the gorgeous Dr Theo Harrison, she is strongly tempted to stay . . .

JO BARTLETT

ST. FINBAR'S CROSS

Complete and Unabridged

LINFORD
Leicester

First published in Great Britain in 2016

First Linford Edition
published 2017

A catalogue record for this book is available
from the British Library.

ISBN 978–1–4448–3362–1

1

Claudia woke up with a start as the train came to an abrupt halt. The view outside her window was obscured by the early evening mists beginning to roll across the Devon countryside, but it was clear they hadn't yet reached the station at St. Finbar's Cross.

'Are you all right? It was a bit of a sudden stop, sorry.'

She looked up at the guard standing in front of her, his ruddy cheeks giving him a friendly appearance.

'I'm fine. Thank you.' She returned his smile — it would have been hard not to: he had one of those faces. 'I was just wondering why we've stopped?'

'A cow on the line.' He had a deep West Country accent, and his matter-of-fact tone convinced Claudia she must have misheard. Being a city girl, she'd heard plenty of excuses for late trains. Leaves on the line, and even the wrong type of snow, but never a *cow*.

'Did you say a *cow*?'

'That's right.' He winked, clearly amused by the look of astonishment that must have crossed her face. 'It happens from time to time round here, but don't worry, it won't hold you up for very long.'

'That's good to hear.' Claudia spoke softly as the guard moved off down the train to warn other passengers of the slight delay. Glancing out of the window, there was no denying how beautiful the countryside was in this part of the world. The combination of dirty train windows and the closing mists of the afternoon only added to the romantic look of the rolling hills. Her mother would have hated it, called it 'the back of beyond' or something equally derogatory.

All the more reason for me to love it. Keeping her gaze firmly fixed out of the window, it seemed an age until the train began to move again and it was a relief

2

when the train finally made its approach to St. Finbar's Cross station. Any delay to starting this new life she'd chosen seemed symbolic somehow, as if she might be making the wrong decision.

Claudia stood up to collect her bags from the rack above her head. Despite the long train journey, her dark blonde hair was still tightly coiled into a careful knot at the nape of her neck. Her appearance at odds with most of the other passengers: casual clothing appeared the order of the day, and she suddenly felt conspicuous in her fitted black suit. By the time she lifted her luggage onto the platform, most of her fellow passengers were already hurrying out of the station.

'Excuse me!' she called after one of the remaining passengers. 'Is there anywhere here I can hire a car?'

'Sorry, you'll be lucky to get a taxi round here, let alone a hire car.' The man looked from her to her bags, and back again. 'Where are you headed?'

'The Golden Fleece Hotel.' Claudia could almost hear her mother's voice inside her head, asking for the tenth time what had possessed her to accept a locum's post in such an obvious backwater, when she could have so many excellent opportunities back at one of the hospitals in Manchester.

'I can offer you a lift.' He looked her up and down again. 'Although I'm afraid my car might not be your type of thing.'

'Thank you, but I don't think I . . . ' Claudia paused, unsure how to phrase the sentence without appearing offensive. It wasn't the thought of a less than luxurious vehicle that put her off, but she wasn't about to risk getting in a car with a complete stranger. Years of living in the centre of a big city and too many experiences of peering at *Crimewatch* from behind a cushion had heightened her natural caution.

'It's no problem if you'd rather not.' He grinned at her response. 'The Golden Fleece is only about half a mile down the road. You can't miss it, just turn right out of the station and keep walking until you see it.'

'That sounds straightforward enough.' Claudia struggled with her luggage, the strap of her bag slipping off her shoulder as she picked up the first suitcase. Maybe she should accept a lift. Glancing at the stranger, she considered his offer again. He didn't look like a serial killer — but, then again, weren't those always the ones to watch?

'You'll never manage all that.' He turned to speak to her as she attempted to follow him out of the station. She had to change over the suitcases in each hand before she even reached the ticket barrier. It was going to be a very long half-mile walk. 'Are you *sure* I can't give you a lift, or at least drop your cases off for you?' He gestured towards a battered old Land Rover, which looked as though it had recently played chicken with a tank and come off much worse.

'Thank you.' Claudia shook her head. 'But I think I'll enjoy the air. I've been cooped up on trains all the way from

Manchester, so the walk will do me good.' Hopefully it sounded more convincing to him than it did to her. After all, what person in their right mind wanted to walk half a mile with two suitcases in heels that suddenly seemed like a ridiculous choice of footwear? It was quite likely this man would be one of her patients; and, from the state of his Land Rover, piled high with animal feed and a saddle propped up on the passenger seat, he'd be visiting her for a tetanus injection before long.

'Well, if you're sure.' He hesitated for a moment, before giving a half-shrug. 'I hope you enjoy the walk.'

The engine of his old car roared to life with surprising ease and, as it disappeared, a bitter wind whipped the hem of her skirt. Despite the sudden blast of cold, it was the beauty of St. Finbar's Cross that took her breath away. Stone cottages dotted both sides of the road that ran into the village, and it was like walking through the middle of a picture postcard.

The Golden Fleece Hotel was in the centre of the village's main street, and Claudia sagged with relief when she finally made it to the entrance, which was well-lit and inviting. It was a combined hotel and inn, but once inside, the only sign of life appeared to be a group of men gathered by the bar.

Standing by the small reception desk, she drummed her fingers with impatience. One of the men at the bar glanced up briefly. He stood out from the others, taller and younger than the rest of them, but there was something else that Claudia couldn't put her finger on until he smiled. It was the man from the station whose offer of a lift she'd turned down. He said something to the rest of the group and a couple of them looked in her direction. Claudia turned away, feigning unnatural interest in the fire regulations notice which was posted above the reception desk. She sighed; she didn't really need all this. It had been a long journey and all she wanted to do was kick off her shoes and relax with a cup of tea. Turning back towards the bar, she saw that the man from the station was walking towards her. He had a fashionably rumpled look, and dark-green eyes which couldn't have matched his thick, roll-neck sweater more closely if it had been a deliberate ploy.

'You made it okay, then?' He gave her a wry smile, the unspoken message being that she'd walked all that way and struggled with her bags for no reason at all.

'Claudia Taylor.' She didn't move to shake his hand. 'I believe I've been booked into the hotel.'

'Is that right?' He leant across the reception desk and picked up the diary.

'Oh yes, looks like you're in here.' He reached up to unhook a key from behind the desk. She'd assumed he was a farm worker when she'd seen him at the train station, not a hotel porter. His customer service skills were a bit on the casual side, but maybe that was what life was like in a place like this. It was going to take some getting used to. 'Theo, by the way. I'll take you up to your room.'

'Thank you, Theo.' Claudia looked at him levelly, tiredness starting to try her patience. 'Do you always keep customers waiting this long?'

'Not as a rule, it can be bad for business.' He flashed his disarming grin again. 'In fact, it can be fatal.' Claudia didn't acknowledge his comment. If he was going to talk in riddles, she wasn't going to rise to it. It was probably some in-joke that he had with his friends at the bar, who he clearly couldn't wait to get back to.

Following Theo up two flights of narrow winding stairs, she was suddenly glad she'd paid such avid attention to the fire regulations and escape route. Finally stopping outside an attic room at the top of the pub, he unlocked the door revealing a welcoming space that spread out like the TARDIS behind its deceiving outer facade. There were two armchairs in one corner and a fireplace at the back of the room which had a neat pile of evenly cut logs stacked up beside it.

'It's beautiful,' Claudia breathed, surprised at her own delight.

'Yes it is.' He showed no signs or leaving and it took her a moment or two to realise why — he was clearly waiting for a tip.

'Here, please, take this.' She pressed a couple of pound coins into his hand.

'No I couldn't!' His eyebrows shot up as he stepped away from her continued attempts to foist money on him.

'Why ever not?' Surely he didn't expect more than that? He'd hardly been able to drag himself away from the bar to do his job as it was.

'Because it wouldn't look good for me to take money from my new locum!' Theo laughed as the heat of a blush flooded right up to Claudia's hairline. 'Didn't I mention I'm Theo Harrison? *Doctor* Theo Harrison?' He adopted an innocent expression, although the effect was spoilt by the fact he seemed to find the whole incident hilarious.

'I'm sorry.' She offered the apology, although she suspected he'd done it on purpose, probably to punish her for being too proud to accept his lift. Maybe she was far more of her mother's daughter than she wanted to admit; a thought that did absolutely nothing to cheer her up.

'Don't be, I'm not in the least offended.'

'So do you often stand in for the porter here?' Maybe it was a family business and he stepped in to help when he wasn't soothing the needs of his patients at the medical centre in St. Finbar's Cross.

'Not that often. The Smithsons who run the place are out for the evening and their son, Paul, was down in the cellar when you arrived.' Theo made it sound like the most normal thing in the world for him to carry visitors' cases up several flight of stairs. 'I'll see you at the surgery in the morning.' He moved out into the corridor, pulling the door towards him as he spoke and she resisted the urge to apologise again. This was a new start and she'd promised herself she'd stop apologising so much. It was a hard habit to break, though, when you were clearly such a disappointment to one of the people who was supposed to love you most.

2

St. Finbar's Cross Medical Centre was situated in a large converted house on the outskirts of the village. In a field behind it was a large chalk cross carved out of the hillside, which gave the village its name. Claudia had read all about the local legend when she'd researched the village prior to accepting the locum's post. The cross was said to bring good luck and inspiration to anyone who took the time and trouble to climb the hill, sit in the centre part of it and make their wish. She didn't believe in all that sort of stuff herself, she had too much of a scientific background, but there was something charming about the idea all the same.

Walking up the drive to the medical centre, she noticed the clapped-out Land Rover parked haphazardly outside. It was a fresh autumn morning and the waiting room was bathed in sunlight as Claudia entered the building. Behind the reception desk was a woman in her early twenties with almost white blonde hair. She was cradling a mug of tea and chatting animatedly to another woman, who was checking through a pile of paperwork on the desk.

'Hi!' The receptionist looked up and noticed Claudia approaching. 'You must be the new locum? I'd recognise you anywhere from Theo's description.' She put down the mug of tea and smiled. 'You've made quite an impression there.'

'Have I? Claudia flushed slightly. 'It's nice to meet you . . . ?'

'Sorry, I'm Stacie Foster, and this is our brilliant practice nurse, Helen Edwards.' Claudia shook both their hands in turn, grateful for the friendly welcome. Coming down from Manchester, she'd been nervous about the reaction she'd receive in such a small place. Thankfully both the medical centre itself and her new colleagues appeared welcoming.

'I'm afraid we won't be easing you

14

into it Dr Taylor.' Stacie indicated the computer screen in front of her. 'I'll get you all logged-in in your consulting room, so you can access the patients' notes and then you can start reviewing their details before they begin to arrive. Can I get you a cup of tea before we get going?' She smiled apologetically as Claudia nodded her head.

'That would be great thanks, Stacie. White with no sugar and, please, call me Claudia. The only time colleagues call me Dr Taylor is when I've done something to upset them!' She laughed and another more distant memory sprang to mind. 'In fact, the only time I've been called by my full name, Claudia Hermione Taylor, was when I'd done something to upset my mother.' Perhaps she was moving on at last, she could mention her mother's name and even hint at the tension between them without getting upset. Maybe time and distance would be the solution after all.

'I'll know I'm in trouble, then, if you call me Nurse Edwards.' Helen lifted the hatch separating the reception desk from the waiting room. 'I'll give you a quick guided tour of the practice while Stacie puts the kettle on. Although you might need to prescribe yourself something after tasting her tea!' Helen laughed at the mock-affronted look on Stacie's face and led Claudia through to the office to start the tour. By the time they reached Helen's room, Claudia had run out of questions to ask about how the surgery ran, what services they offered and where the nearest pharmacy was. But there was still one question left.

'Is Theo about?' She'd expected him to show her around, anticipated his easy manner. Although she wouldn't admit it, even to herself, she'd been looking forward to seeing him again. He was different from the medics she'd mixed with, growing up in a household where all her parents' friends worked in the sector, and then, later, in the jobs she'd had in Manchester. She didn't know many of them who'd appreciate being

16

mistaken for the night porter or being offered two pounds as a tip. If she wanted to avoid turning into a version of her mother, she could do with learning how to lighten up; maybe working with Theo would help with that.

'Yes, he's here,' Helen replied. 'He's already in his room, going through the budget. He hates cutting corners, but it has to be done somewhere.' Helen sounded wistful. Everyone working in the NHS knew full well it was a fact of life in these days of austerity cuts, but that didn't make it any easier to take.

'He made an early start.'

'They've been getting earlier and earlier since his divorce. Lately, it's like he's married to his work . . . ' Helen clamped a hand over her mouth, as if regretting saying so much.

'Have you worked together long?' Claudia was glad Helen had mentioned his divorce; at least she was less likely to put her foot in it that way.

'Since he set up the practice. He's

great to work with, but you'll find that out for yourself.' Helen returned the new ophthalmoscope, which she'd shown Claudia earlier, to the drawer of her desk. 'Anyway, let me show you through to your room, I'm sure you want to get started and Stacie will be in with that tea, and her expert tuition on the computer system, before you know it.'

For the second time in two days, Claudia was delighted by a room hidden behind a deceptively ordinary door. The consulting room she'd be using was large and well equipped, dominated by a beautiful oak desk and a state-of-the-art computer system. Best of all were the long French windows, which were closed but led out on to a small terrace overlooking the gardens behind the medical centre with a clear view of St. Finbar's Cross.

'I'll leave you to get on.' Helen smiled warmly. 'I'm sure you'll be really happy while you're here. Just let me know if you need anything.'

'Thanks Helen. I can't think of a

nicer setting, or one more different from my last job.' St. Finbar's Cross was a world away from anywhere that Claudia had ever known.

Stacie arrived with the promised cup of tea, which was left to get cold as she whizzed Claudia through the surgery's IT system. Luckily it was all pretty easy to follow and she soon had access to her patients' notes for the morning surgery. Disappearing with the promise of a second cup of tea, Stacie was gone. She was a bit of a whirlwind, but Claudia suspected it was Stacie who kept the surgery running like clockwork; good receptionists were the backbone of surgeries of this size.

Keen to get to work, Claudia started on the morning's case notes. She was so engrossed in one patient's history of endometriosis, and her resulting infertility, that she didn't look up as Stacie came back in.

'Thank so much, you're a marvel. Hot tea and IT tutoring, is there no end to your talents?' Claudia glanced up as she finished speaking realising too late that it wasn't Stacie who'd come in, but a very amused-looking Theo.

'Sorry to disappoint you Claudia.' His green eyes twinkled with merriment and she constantly seemed to be on the back foot with him. 'But I haven't come bearing tea, only to wish you good luck for your first morning.' He sat on the edge of her desk. 'Are you getting to grips with finding everything on the system?' Leaning across her, so that they almost touched, he clicked a button on her keyboard, the list of her patients for the morning appearing on the screen. 'Ah, you're seeing Matthew King this morning, it's an interesting case.' Theo looked serious for once.

'Something I should know more about before I see him?'

'Yes, I think a bit of background may help.' Theo ran his hand through his unruly black hair. 'He's the porter from the Golden Fleece Hotel, but he's got a personality disorder.'

'Really?' Claudia moved to access

Matthew King's notes. This did sound like an interesting case — one her mother might even appreciate, despite her feelings about general practice.

'Yes, he keeps thinking he's a doctor!' For about two seconds Theo kept a straight face, before breaking into that already familiar laugh of his. She'd worked with some colleagues back in Manchester for years and hadn't heard them laugh as much as she'd heard him laugh in less than twenty-four hours. Maybe country life really was less stressful, if Theo's demeanour was anything to go by.

'Thank you, Doctor.' Claudia tried to look indignant, but she couldn't help smiling. 'I'll be sure to seek your advice. After all, you're the expert on these things.' She pretended to push him off the edge off the desk and he held up his hands in response.

'Sorry, I couldn't resist! Seriously, though, have a good morning and welcome to the team.' He stood up. 'I'm only next door if you need me.' As he opened the door of the consulting room, Claudia could already hear Stacie talking to the patients beginning to arrive for morning surgery. This was it. The real start of her new life as a country GP.

* * *

The first half of the morning passed in busy routine for Claudia. Autumn seemed to be bringing with it the usual rash of colds, sore throats and ear infections. Eleven o'clock arrived with Claudia's first interesting case of the day. She glanced quickly through Mr Grainger's notes as he entered the consulting room with his wife.

'What can I do for you then, Mr Grainger?' Claudia smiled at the elderly couple as they took their seats on the other side of the desk. They looked so sweet, holding hands the whole time.

'It's my legs again, Doctor; all night they're twitching. We've tried all the life-style changes Dr Hall recommended, but none of them do any good.' Mr Grainger nodded his head towards his wife. 'It's not fair on Betty, I'm keeping her awake all night too.'

Claudia looked down at the notes again. 'I see from your records that Dr Hall prescribed some sleeping tablets for your restless legs, were they any help?' She smiled sympathetically at Mr Grainger as he sighed.

'Not really, Doctor. I mean I was out like a light and didn't stir once, but my legs still thrashed about and Betty didn't have the benefit of the tablets.'

Mrs Grainger leant across the desk and added conspiratorially, 'The other doctor suggested we sleep separately, but we've been married fifty-five years and we don't like to sleep alone.' Her cheeks coloured slightly as her husband nodded in agreement.

'Well, I'm sure we can find a more satisfactory solution than that.' Silently cursing her predecessor's insensitivity, Claudia read through the notes again. 'I notice that Dr Hall carried out blood and circulation tests to rule out anything more serious?' She looked at Mr Grainger and smiled. 'Did he explain much to you about the condition?'

It was Mrs Grainger who responded to Claudia's question first.

'Oh yes, he said it wasn't serious and no-one really knows what causes it, but it can run in families.' Mrs Grainger smiled suddenly and added, 'My daughter-in-law says if our son Terry gets it, she'll make him sleep in the shed!' Claudia couldn't help laughing.

'I think we'll prescribe a different course of action for your husband, don't you?' She turned back to the computer. 'I'm going to prescribe you Horizant, it's a drug that was developed from anti-seizure medication.' Turning back to the couple, Claudia didn't miss their look of alarm. 'Don't worry, there shouldn't be any side effects from this drug, other than perhaps a little drowsiness, but you can let me know if there's anything that concerns you. Most people find that by taking one tablet a day the symptoms disappear within a week or two.' Claudia took the prescription from the printer and handed it to Mr Grainger. 'Of course, it isn't actually a cure but, if it works for you, it will allow you to control your symptoms indefinitely.'

Mrs Grainger squeezed Claudia's hand affectionately. 'Thank you, dear; we've been sleeping apart for a couple of weeks now and I can't wait to get back to normal. I've had no one to warm my feet on when it gets cold!' She winked at Claudia and released her hand. 'Come on, Bob, let's get down the chemist's and get this thing sorted once and for all.'

Claudia finished updating Mr Grainger's notes as they left the consulting room. There'd been so much affection between the couple and they'd reminded Claudia of her grandparents. She still missed them, especially her grandmother, the one person she'd always been able to turn to when she needed unconditional love. Maybe that's why things had come to a head with her parents in the end, their relationship no longer bearable without her grandmother around to soften the edges. She wondered if Mr and Mrs Grainger's son, Terry, realised how lucky he was to have parents like them. Shaking off thoughts of her own family, she called through her next patient.

* * *

The rest of the morning was just as busy and, when her extension buzzed just before lunch-time, Claudia was shocked by just how much time had passed.

'I've just had a phone call from Chrissie Denton.' It was Stacie's soft Devon accent. 'She was supposed to be your last patient of the morning, but she's been held up. I've re-scheduled her for 4.30 this afternoon.'

'That's fine, thanks, Stacie.' Chrissie was the patient suffering infertility and Claudia was glad that she'd have more than the planned ten minutes to devote to the consultation.

She spent a few minutes checking her list for the afternoon. Just after one o'clock, the sunshine, which had been battling to prevail all day, finally gave way to rain.

Claudia shut down the computer and wandered through to the practice's kitchen, which was situated next to Helen's office. Theo was already seated at the kitchen table, steadily working his way through a huge pile of doorstep-width sandwiches.

'Have you had a good morning?' Theo looked relieved as she nodded. 'Anything interesting?'

'Oh, you know, just a couple who've been married for fifty-odd years and who wanted some help in the bedroom department.' Claudia poured herself a coffee and smiled as Theo raised his eyebrows, before offering an explanation. 'Restless legs.'

Taking a seat opposite Theo, he pushed the plate of sandwiches towards her.

'Do you want one? Not exactly tea at

the Ritz, but Stacie likes everyone to be well fed!' Theo indicated one of the huge roughly cut sandwiches. 'We keep telling her we can bring our own, but she runs every inch of this place and it seems even a sandwich service isn't beyond her means. Although the choice is cheese or ham and that's about it, but we do occasionally get tuna if she's feeling like a walk on the wild side.'

'Thanks.' Determined not to have a repeat of the day before, after turning down his offer of a lift, she took half a sandwich from the pile. 'How about you, have you had a good morning?' Claudia pushed a loose tendril of blonde hair behind her ear as she spoke.

'The highlight of my morning was a case of chicken pox.' Theo smiled across at her. 'Although sharing a lunch table with you is a big improvement on the last guy.'

'Another locum?'

'Yes, Dr Hall was here for three months but he didn't have the most sympathetic of bedside manners.'

'And you're not looking to make an appointment for a permanent post here?' It wasn't something Claudia was after, she wasn't ready to settle down to in one place just yet. She had too many issues of her own to work through first, but it seemed odd for the surgery to employ a series of locums.

'My previous partner, Dr Bramwell, was originally planning to come home after three months' sabbatical with a VSO programme in Ghana. Only he didn't plan on falling in love with the place and the woman who ran the hotel he was staying at. So he's decided not to come home at all. Dr Hall wasn't someone I wanted to keep on any longer, so that's why I arranged with the agency for another locum, until we can appoint the right person. The job's advertised on the BMJ website, if you're interested?'

Claudia gave a non-committal smile, her reasons for wanting to stay working as a locum were not something she wanted to get into. 'That must have been hard on you, keeping the place running with your partner gone?'

'I haven't had a day off during those three months, put it like that.' He looked at her for a moment. 'But sometimes work helps you get through all the other stuff. Do you know what I mean?'

'I do.' For a moment she thought he might say something about the divorce, but he didn't. She could have told him why work had been her salvation for years, but that wasn't a conversation for her first day at work, or probably ever. Some things were best kept to yourself.

★ ★ ★

After lunch, Claudia got straight back to work. Her case-load for the afternoon was so heavy she didn't have time to think too much. She was running about fifteen minutes late by the time her last patient of the day, Chrissie Denton, left the consulting room. Theo was waiting when she went out into the reception area to speak to Stacie about some repeat appointments she wanted to schedule.

'Everything all right?' He looked up as she approached Stacie's desk.

'Yes, fine.' She nodded in response. It had been a good day overall. 'Although I do need your advice.'

'I'm flattered, Dr Taylor.' Theo teased her. 'You seemed to be managing so well, I thought I might become redundant.'

'I don't think there's any danger of that,' she reassured him. 'I gather from speaking to patients today that you've got quite a fan club around here.'

'And it's not just his patients that love him.' Stacie smiled up at her and shot Theo a look.

'You're the one they rave about the most.' He nudged Stacie as he spoke. 'I think it's because they're so surprised when a doctor's receptionist is actually nice to them!'

'Stacie has certainly looked after me

wonderfully today.' Claudia spoke as she watched her two new colleagues; trying to work out if their relationship was based on friendly banter, or if there might be something more to it than that.

'You've been no trouble at all.' Stacie spoke in a stage whisper. 'Not like that Dr Hall!'

'It's been fun, actually, but it still feels like it's been a long day. Must be all that new information to get to grips with.'

'Monday surgery will do that to you!' Theo grabbed his car keys from the table. 'Come on, I'll give you a lift to the hotel and perhaps I can give you that advice you wanted?'

* * *

Claudia climbed into Theo's battered Land Rover, which looked more like the type of car that a country vet would feel at home in.

It was a very short journey to the

hotel and when they pulled up outside, she was still outlining the details of Chrissie Denton's case.

'She's been in constant pain.' Claudia was able to lower her voice as Theo switched of the ignition and the loud chugging of the Land Rover finally stopped. 'It's put a terrible strain on her marriage and now they want to try fertility treatment, but she's worried that if it fails it could mean the end for them.' During the consultation, Claudia hadn't been sure what to advise. She knew that getting pregnant could ease the pain of endometriosis, and she'd discussed that with Chrissie, but she also aware that when fertility treatment failed it could have a massive effect on even the strongest of marriages.

'Was her husband with her when you talked about their options?' Theo asked as he turned to face her. When she shook her head, he sighed. 'I think it's important that he's involved in the decision. If he comes to her next consultation, you can let them know the odds of the fertility treatment working. That way they can weigh up the decision together and he won't feel cut off. Fertility treatment can put marriages under strain, but I think it's a lack of communication or one person making a decision without consulting the other that's often at the root of that. That's a recipe for distaste in any marriage, whether it involves fertility treatment or not.' He sounded like he was speaking from experience and Claudia found herself wondering about his situation again. Not that it was any of her business. She didn't want anyone prying into her life, so she had no right to ask him any questions.

'Thanks for the advice.' She hastily leapt on to the pavement. 'I'll see you tomorrow then.'

'Goodnight.' Theo's reply was almost drowned out by the chugging of the engine as he restarted his old car and pulled away.

3

Claudia had wondered whether the weekends in St. Finbar's Cross were when her mother's doom-laden premonition might come true, and she would find herself bored rigid. Only Juliet clearly hadn't reckoned on how the people of St. Finbar's Cross would welcome her daughter. She'd received a number of invitations for her first weekend in the village, including one from Helen, the practice nurse, to join her on her training for a half-marathon. It wasn't something that Claudia would have done back in Manchester, the traffic and the crowds made running on the treadmill an easier prospect, but she'd been tempted by the beauty of the Devon countryside, so Saturday morning was spent jogging on farm tracks and down a bridle path that had taken them through some stunning woodland, which had turned to shades of gold and orange as summer finally gave in fully to autumn.

On Sunday, Claudia had promised to meet Stacie to go bowling in the nearby town of Bassington. It was nice to get to know her colleagues and Theo had promised to meet them for a coffee in the afternoon too. If she'd been looking for a permanent position, the job at the medical centre might have tempted her. As it was, she just didn't feel ready to take on any long-term commitments. Maybe it was the doubt her mother had put in her mind, or maybe that even Devon didn't feel as though it would be far enough away from her sniping. How her father had lived with it for all these years, she would never know.

'Are you ready for this?' Stacie wound down the window of her car, as Claudia crossed the car park of The Golden Fleece Inn. 'I hope you don't mind, but I brought my mum and brother along too.'

'Not at all.' Claudia could already see

the little boy's face, pressed excitedly up against the window of the backseat of the car. He had a shock of black hair and a smile that could have melted the hardest of hearts. He only looked about seven or eight, so there was a considerable age gap between him and his sister.

'This is my mum, Nicola,' Stacie started the introductions as Claudia climbed into the passenger seat, 'and my little brother Danny.'

'Nice to meet you both.' Claudia turned in her seat to greet Stacie's family and was rewarded with another megawatt smile from the little boy.

'Sorry that we've gatecrashed your day out, Claudia.' Nicola squeezed her shoulder and it was clear where Stacie got her friendly disposition from. 'But Danny was so excited at the prospect of meeting you and, when Stacie mentioned bowling, there was no holding him back.'

'It's actually a huge relief that you're coming with us.' Claudia laughed at the expression which crossed Stacie's face in response. 'Not because Stacie and I would run out of things to talk about, but having Danny with us means I've got an excuse to keep the guides up at the bowling alley. Otherwise my ball is likely to disappear down the gulley every single time, whilst I try for a new strike out record.'

'You and me both.' Nicola squeezed her shoulder again. 'Stacie was right about you, I think you'll fit in perfectly round here.'

★   ★   ★

Danny turned out to be the only one of the four of them who didn't need the help of the guards to stop his bowling ball disappearing into the gulley. He was a whizz at knocking down the pins, even though his slim build made it look as though he was going to topple over every time he picked up the ball.

'How did he get so good at this?' Claudia watched as the little boy knocked down all of his pins again, smiling when he leapt up and punched the air in response, before hurtling towards his mum for a celebratory hug.

'He can't always join in with other sports.' Stacie sighed. 'He's got cystic fibrosis and if he takes part in exercise that's too vigorous he can end up breathless or have a coughing fit that scares the heck out of all of us. He's really hard to slow down, though, and he wants to do everything, but bowling is one of the options we feel more comfortable with.'

'It must be hard not to want to wrap him up in cotton wool.' Claudia looked at Danny again, now trying to show his mother how to bowl a ball. If anything Nicola was even worse at bowling than Claudia and that took some doing.

'It is, especially when he's just like an average eight-year-old boy in most ways. He likes nothing better than getting covered in mud or into mischief with the rest of his friends.' Stacie shrugged and she suddenly looked much older. 'It's always been just Danny, Mum and I since he was born and my stepfather couldn't cope with his diagnosis. I expect the poor boy feels like he's got two over-protective mothers. I was nearly sixteen when he was born and my dad died when I was only five, so mum's had a really tough time of it over the years. We're like the three musketeers but sometimes I think he'd like us to back off a bit.'

'He looks pretty happy to me.' Claudia looked over to where Danny was high-fiving his mother, as she finally managed to knock down some pins. 'He's a great kid.'

'He is and we're blessed to have him.' Stacie gave her a wry smile. 'It's just a shame his father is too self-centred to make any time for his son. Some people shouldn't be parents.'

'I couldn't agree more.' Claudia was tempted to tell her new friend why she felt so strongly about some people's capacity to parent too, but she had nothing to complain about really. Stacie's little brother was struggling with a serious illness and his family were suffering with the knowledge too. Claudia's own dysfunctional relationship, with an emotionally distant mother, was nothing in comparison.

* * *

'Can we have fish and chips?' Danny was petitioning everyone who would listen for his favourite dinner.

'Well I think the winner should get to choose, so I can't see why not.' Claudia looked towards Nicola. 'If it's okay with your mum and Stacie that is?'

'Mum said the guest should get to choose.' Danny was sporting that disarming grin of his again. 'So if you say it's okay, we can do it!'

'I'll text Theo and tell him to meet us at Sea Salt.' Stacie smiled. 'They do the best fish and chips in Devon, don't they Dan?'

'More like the world!' Dan skipped

on ahead of them. They'd decided to leave the car in the car park at the bowling alley and walk down to the sea front for something to eat. Bassington was only about ten minutes in the car from St. Finbar's Cross but it was much bigger and had less of the charm of the village that Claudia was already thinking of as home. It was dangerous to think that way, though, and she'd never prove her mother wrong if she stayed in the first job that came along.

By the time they reached the restaurant, Theo was already waiting outside and, as soon as he saw him, Danny picked up his pace again and hurtled into the doctor's arms.

'Whoa, champ, if you get much bigger, you'll have to be the one who catches me.' Theo swung the little boy round. In truth he had the typical slight build of a child with cystic fibrosis but, from the look on his face, he clearly liked the idea that before much longer he'd be strong enough to lift a grown man. Theo obviously knew Danny well enough to understand that; and Claudia found herself wondering if there was more to his relationship with Stacie than met the eye. There'd been no real hint of it at the surgery, other than their jokey relationship, but he wouldn't have been the first doctor to fall for his receptionist.

'So did this young man keen up his unbeaten record?' Theo raised an eyebrow and Nicola nodded in response.

'He beat us hollow, like he always does. We were hoping Claudia might be the one to challenge him, but . . . '

'It's alright, you can tell it like it is.' Claudia's eyes met Theo's briefly. 'I was useless.'

'I somehow doubt that.' He finally disentangled himself from the little boy and opened the door to the restaurant. 'Shall we go inside?'

Sea Salt was a modern fish and chip restaurant with scrubbed pine tables and a laid-back atmosphere. It was a long way from eating cod straight out of the paper, though, with a menu that included everything from salt and pepper squid to garlic scallops. The far wall of the restaurant was made from a sheet of curved glass that directly overlooked the sea. Danny was obviously a boy of sophisticated tastes.

'Ah Danny, it's good to see you.' One of the waiters came over and greeted them with a smile. 'Are you going straight to the tank or do you want to look at the menu first?'

'You know I always have the goujons!' Danny looked at the waiter as if he'd asked the most obvious question in the world. 'I'm going to have a look at the fish. Can you tell me when it's ready please?' He turned round and grinned at his mum, who was standing next to Claudia.

'Of course, sweetheart.' Without another backward look, Danny made his way straight over to the huge fish tank at the far end of the restaurant, where tropical fish swam in an environment bathed with coloured lights. 'That's why he really comes here, not just for the upmarket fish fingers,' Nicola confided to Claudia as they took they seats.

'How are the plans for the fundraiser going?' Theo looked up from his menu and Claudia felt momentarily left out. She'd never lived in the sort of community that held fundraisers, but from the animated look on Stacie's face it was set to be a bit event in St. Finbar's Cross.

'It's going well, but we're still looking for donations for the auction of promises.' Stacie grinned, suddenly looking very much like her little brother. 'Have you got any specialist services you can offer?'

'Nothing that isn't already available on the NHS!' Theo laughed. 'I could offer to do some gardening, but since I can barely tell the difference between a daffodil and a tulip, that might not be a good idea!'

'What's the fundraiser for?' Claudia wanted to help if she could. She might not be planning to stay around for ever, but that didn't mean she didn't want to get involved at all.

'It's for Danny.' Stacie shot a furtive look in her little brother's direction, but he still had his face pressed up against the fish tank. 'He's always wanted to go to America to swim with dolphins and some of the villagers had the idea of raising the funds for him to go. There's already been a quiz night and a fun run, so they're hoping they'll have enough after the auction and the fete.'

'I wish we could have just done it ourselves.' Nicola looked embarrassed. 'But money's a bit tight and I haven't really been able to work regular hours since Danny was born, especially as I need to be with him when he's not well. I don't know what I'd do without Stacie.' She reached over to squeeze her daughter's hand.

'You won't ever have to.'

'Is there anything I can do to help?' Claudia felt another pang of recognition about her relationship with her own mother. Stacie and Nicola would do anything for each other. It was obvious and exactly how family life should be; only it didn't always turn out that way.

'Is there anything you could offer for the auction of promises?' Theo gave her another of his questioning looks.

'Well I can cook pretty well.' Claudia didn't want to explain how she'd come to be such a good cook, spending so much time with the help her mother had hired growing up meant that she'd developed a whole range of skills that her mother didn't feel the need to develop. Betsy had been a cordon bleu cook and had worked for Claudia's family for about ten years, so she could whip up an impressive five-course meal from scratch. 'So maybe I can offer to be someone's personal chef.'

'I'd bid on that.' Theo looked surprised at her offer, he obviously didn't have her down as a domestic goddess.

'That's brilliant, Claudia.' Stacie drummed her fingers on the table as she spoke. 'There must be something you can do, Theo. I'm offering make-overs and Helen's doing Indian head massages, you don't want to be the only one from the surgery letting the side down.'

'No pressure then.' He looked thoughtful for a moment. 'How about if I offer a riding lesson.'

'I think you'd need insurance for that.' Nicola sighed. 'I've looked into a few things like that and let's just say the red tape doesn't make any of this easy.'

'I'd love to learn to ride.' Claudia couldn't supress her excitement at the thought and she suddenly knew how Danny felt when he saw the fish tank. She'd always wanted to learn to ride, but her mother had insisted it would distract from her studies. The only extra-curricular activities that Juliet had wanted to support involved a personal tutor to improve her grades. Like most little girls, Claudia had dreamt of having a pony. The only time she'd been able to ride was on a pony trekking holiday that her beloved grandmother had taken her on in Wales. It was one of the best memories of her entire childhood and the thought of riding through the Devon countryside sounded irresistible. 'How about I bid on it outside the auction, so that we don't need to worry about insurance. I'm more than happy to make a sizeable donation to the fund.'

'That's a brilliant idea!' Stacie clapped her hands together. 'If you don't mind, Theo?'

'I couldn't think of a nicer way to spend the day.' Theo held Claudia's gaze for a moment and she was suddenly much more confident that there was nothing going on between him and Stacie. Not that it mattered to Claudia of course, they were just friends and she certainly wasn't looking for any more than that from him. After all, she'd be leaving St. Finbar's Cross before long, but there was no harm in enjoying life here whilst it lasted.

4

It was Claudia's third week at St. Finbar's Medical Centre before she met the surgery's most formidable patient. Mrs Jessop came with a health warning of her own. She visited the surgery most weeks, according to Theo, and she always asked for him. However, he was fully booked on the Friday morning and Mrs Jessop apparently couldn't wait until the following week to see a doctor — so Claudia found herself coming face to face with a living legend.

Mrs Jessop was exactly as Theo had described her. Old-fashioned, with her hat firmly secured by a pearl-topped hat pin to her iron-grey hair, a clue to the iron will that apparently lurked beneath the heavily patterned floral dress she was wearing.

'Right, Doctor.' Mrs Jessop addressed

Claudia as if she were talking to a young child. 'I've come to see you about my leg.' She indicated the offending limb and then sat back, as if she'd provided more than enough information for a diagnosis.

'What actually seems to be the problem?' Claudia prompted, supressing a smile as she heard Mrs Jessop's heavy sigh; it was another of the tactics Theo had warned her about.

'Well, *I'm* convinced the problem is a cancerous tumour, but . . . ' Mrs Jessop paused and stared at Claudia meaningfully. ' . . . as the doctor, I was assuming *you* would tell *me* what the problem is.'

Unfazed by Mrs Jessop's attitude, Claudia leant back slightly in her chair, grateful that Theo had forewarned her. 'Perhaps I should put it another way. What symptoms are you are experiencing? Do you have any pain?'

'No pain, just a huge lump.' Mrs Jessop gave a shuddering sigh. 'I'm sure you know what that means, Doctor, I mean *everyone* does.' Mrs Jessop shook her head, as if she couldn't believe that Claudia hadn't grasped it yet. 'Everyone knows the most dangerous types of lumps are the ones that don't hurt. They just sit quietly, with the cancer growing and don't start to hurt until it's too late to do anything.'

Even after Theo's warning, Claudia was shocked that the woman sitting opposite had all but arranged her own funeral. All this from a self-diagnosis and probably an internet search. Google had a lot to answer for.

'Let's not jump to any conclusions.' Her attempt to reassure the older woman was met with a derisory grunt, which she did her best to ignore. 'Can I take a look at the lump?'

Claudia walked around the desk and Mrs Jessop stood up, hitching up the bottom of her dress to reveal wrinkled stockings; even Nora Batty would have been proud of such fine specimens. Claudia ran her hand gently down Mrs Jessop's leg, but at first she couldn't feel anything more than the slightly lumpy veins that were fairly common in women of a certain age, especially those who'd spent a lot of their working lives on their feet. A quick glance at Mrs Jessop's notes had revealed that she'd been a shopkeeper up until her retirement two years before.

Repeating the examination, Claudia felt it — just at the back of the knee — a soft lump about the size of a tangerine. She'd need to ask a few more questions to be sure, but she was already pretty confident she'd be able to make a swift diagnosis that could put Mrs Jessop's mind at rest.

'Can you feel the lump there *all* the time?' Claudia watched her patient's face as she spoke. Theo had said she visited often, but it was always with symptoms that seemed genuine, even if she did have a tendency to blow them out of proportion.

'No.' Mrs Jessop sounded certain. 'It's a bit strange, now that you mention it. I seem to become aware of the lump during the day, but by the time I'm ready for bed it's usually disappeared and it's not there in the morning either.'

'It's a Baker's cyst.' Claudia spoke as she washed her hands, drying them carefully before returning to sit opposite Mrs Jessop.

'Is it cancerous?' From the tone of her patient's voice, it almost sounded as though she wanted it to be. Theo had said he didn't think she had a serious psychological condition, like Munchausen's, but Claudia suspected that the death of Mrs Jessop's husband the year before had compounded her fears about her own health, which was only to be expected.

'Actually it's completely harmless.' Claudia was trying to tread carefully, but she didn't miss the look of disbelief on Mrs Jessop's face. 'When you crouch down, the lubricant fluid in your knee is being pressurised and squeezed into a pocket at the back of the joint.' Claudia glanced down at Mrs Jessop's notes. 'I notice you've had some back and joint pain too? Dr Harrison told me what a keen gardener you are, have you been doing a lot of weeding lately?'

'Well, yes.' The old lady's response was grudging. 'Though I can't believe that's the cause of it, how can you be so sure?' She seemed almost offended to have been diagnosed with a harmless condition.

'When you're crouching down to do the gardening and weeding during the day, the lump appears. Once you stop crouching down, the fluid gradually flows back into the joint and the lump disappears.' Claudia smiled at Mrs Jessop. 'I'm afraid that there's nothing I can prescribe, except perhaps using a low chair to sit on while you're gardening rather than crouching or kneeling.'

'Thank you Doctor.' Mrs Jessop's tone was abrupt and as she opened the consulting room door she added, 'I don't think I'll take your word for it though, I think it's best if I get another opinion.'

'About what?' Theo's voice made

Claudia jump. He'd been pinning some sort of poster to the noticeboard outside Claudia's consulting room and he was just in time to hear Mrs Jessop's comments. Remarkable timing actually, almost as though he planned it; especially as it was Stacie who usually took care of that sort of thing.

'What was it you wanted a second opinion on Mrs Jessop?' Theo repeated himself patiently, when neither of the women moved to answer him.

'This lump on my leg, if you *must* know.' Mrs Jessop looked pointedly at Claudia. 'This new doctor tells me it's harmless, but I can't see how it can be myself.'

'Let's take a look then, shall we?' Theo gently guided Mrs Jessop back into the consulting room and asked her to repeat her symptoms. After examining her, and questioning her about the times of day when she noticed the lump, he made the same diagnosis as Claudia — it was definitely a Baker's cyst.

'You'll have to take a bit more care of yourself. None of us are getting any younger you know.' Theo smiled, earning himself another one of Mrs Jessop's disdainful looks. 'Take it a bit easier when you're doing that garden of yours.'

'There was something else I wanted to mention too.' Claudia had a horrible feeling that Mrs Jessop wasn't going to like what she had to say much, but it could be the one thing that made a difference to how she was feeling that didn't need any medical intervention. 'I wanted you to take a look at this.' She handed Mrs Jessop a leaflet.

'A befriending service?' The tone of Mrs Jessop's voice did nothing to allay Claudia's fears.

'It says in your notes you mentioned to the previous locum that you felt lonely sometimes, since your husband passed away and with no family nearby?'

'I knew I shouldn't have told that Dr Hall anything, I only mentioned it because I knew he wouldn't stick around long and he caught me on an off day. I don't need all this meddling in my life, thank you very much.' Mrs Jessop huffed loudly, but Claudia noticed her stuff the leaflet into her bag all the same. She could only hope that it didn't end up in the recycling bin the moment Mrs Jessop got home.

'For what it's worth, I think it's a good idea too, Irene.' Theo spoke gently. 'And if you're still worried about the cyst on your leg over the next week or so, you can always come back to see us. But I fully support Dr Taylor's diagnosis that it's completely harmless, if a bit inconvenient.'

'Just like you doctors to stick together,' Mrs Jessop muttered as she finally left the consulting room. 'I'll still be checking my medical books when I get in, don't you worry.'

Claudia wondered briefly just how old those books of Mrs Jessop's were. Still at least she couldn't blame it on Google for once. She turned to Theo and smiled. Maybe she should have been cross that he was checking up on her consultation with Mrs Jessop, in case she couldn't handle it, but it was actually nice to know she had his backing. She was starting to feel more and more a part of the medical centre every day.

'Thanks for that.'

'No problem. I'm just glad that Mrs Jessop lived up to her reputation and that you handled it so well.'

'I think she was a lot more honest with Dr Hall than she'd have us believe. There's no doubt she's feeling lonely sometimes and I think that coming in here to see us is her way of connecting with someone, feeling as if someone still cares about her. That's why I suggested the befriending service.' Claudia felt sorry for her, if that was the case. She needed help alright, but it probably wasn't the kind that a doctor could dispense. Despite the Baker's cyst, Mrs Jessop was fit and well overall and far too young in her mid-sixties to be feeling the way she did about life.

'I've suspected in the past that she'd love to have a diagnosis of something serious, something that needed ongoing treatment.' Theo frowned. 'She uses those medical books of hers to look up illnesses and then makes her symptoms fit. I can't work out whether she's after attention or whether she's just had enough of her life. It's pretty sad either way.'

'Is there anywhere we can refer her to that might help?'

'I've tried suggesting she joins a local bereavement support group and even offered to refer her for counselling.' Theo shook his head. 'I think she said that she'd rather stick pins in her eyes than sit talking to a group of strangers about how she was feeling.'

'I can just imagine her saying that!' Claudia couldn't help smiling at the thought. It was a shame though, as Mrs Jessop would probably have got a lot out of it. Maybe she'd change her mind about joining one of the groups or even make that call to the befriending service, Claudia certainly hoped so.

'And what about you?' Theo raised an eyebrow. 'Are there any local groups I could persuade you to join that might make you want to stay in St. Finbar's Cross for a bit longer?'

'I'm not sure. Maybe if the riding lesson works out?' Claudia kept her tone light, she didn't want to get into a conversation with Theo about why she could never really fit in life in the village, especially when he'd made it so obvious he'd like her to stay. If she didn't have her mother's voice in her head all the time, telling her that it would be a waste of her opportunities, she might even have been tempted by the offer. Being around Theo was no hardship either.

'I'll try my best to make it an unforgettable experience then.' Theo moved back towards the door of her consulting room. 'In the meantime, my sister's been nagging me half to death to take you over to her place for lunch.

She's taken it upon herself to become the unofficial welcoming committee to all newcomers in the village and I'm in trouble for keeping you to myself for so long.'

'Is that what you've been doing?'

'Given half the chance, perhaps I would.' Theo had a relaxed charm that would be all too easy to fall for. He was funny and kind too, but he obviously had a history that would complicate any new relationships. Either way she couldn't get involved with anyone until she'd established her career and proved her mother wrong about the decisions she'd made, but it was hard not to respond when he made comments like that.

⋆　⋆　⋆

Claudia was ready for an early night by the time she got back to the Golden Fleece Inn. The weeks at the surgery flew by, but they were busy and demanding. She had a date with a

David Attenborough documentary about Alaska, which she was excusing as research for the next step in her career, and plans for a Chinese takeaway. Walking through the pub to get to the door which led up to her room, Claudia was surprised to see Stacie sitting on a stool at the bar swinging her legs and nursing a large gin and tonic. Catching sight of her friend's pale face, and against her better judgement, Claudia decided to join Stacie for a drink before heading up to the sanctuary of her room.

'Hi, do you mind if I join you?' Aware that it sounded like a bad chat-up line, Claudia smiled. She'd heard worse, of course, but at least she'd managed to bring a smile to Stacie's face too.

'I could use the company.' Stacie shook her head as she spoke. 'I'm not in the habit of sitting on my own drinking and it's not something I want to get into the habit of, either!'

'Probably a good idea.' Claudia sat down next to her new friend and put a hand on her arm. 'You can tell me to mind my own business altogether if you like, but if you need a listening ear, I'm more than happy to provide one.'

'I've managed to get myself to get myself into a situation that I didn't see coming and now I don't know what to do.' Stacie was shivering, despite the warmth in the pub.

'Sometimes these things seem much worse than they really are, when you're trying to solve them all by yourself.' Claudia knew only too well what it could do to someone to feel as if you didn't have any support, or someone who could act as a sounding board. It was hard to believe that Stacie ever felt that way, though, with a mum like Nicola.

'Can I get you something?' Jennie, the daughter of the Smithson family, who owned the pub, had come over to their table to collect the glass Stacie had already drained.

'I think two coffees are probably best.' Stacie shot Claudia a look as she spoke; at least her friend had realised the one place she definitely wouldn't find an answer was in the bottom of a glass.

'Coming right up.' Jennie sauntered away from the table, not looking as if she was in any particular hurry to get their order. Still, at least that would give them a chance to talk.

'Are you sure you've got time to listen to all of this?' Stacie suddenly looked a lot younger than her years and Claudia wanted to give her a hug, she couldn't imagine what it was that was worrying Stacie so much, but she crossed her fingers under the table, hoping it was nothing to do with Danny.

'Of course, I have. I'm not promising I'll have any of the answers, but I can promise I'll hear you out, whatever it is.'

'Over the summer, I started going out with a guy called Greg, for what was just supposed to be a holiday romance.' She smiled, the memory of it tinging her cheeks with pink. 'But somehow I ended up falling in love.'

'Well on the face of it, that doesn't sound like anything too much to get upset about.' Claudia was well aware that things were often more complicated than they seemed, though.

'Maybe it wouldn't be, but he works as a project manager overseeing hotel renovations for a large chain based in Australia, but they have sites all over the world. He was just finishing a big project in Devon that he was working on when we met, but he's due to go back over there at the end of the month and he wants me to go with him. He's even proposed.' Stacie lifted her left hand off her lap for the first time and placed it on the table, a pretty ruby and diamond ring glittering on her finger as if it was meant to be there.

'But that's fantastic news, congratulations!' Claudia leant across the table to give the younger woman a hug.

'It would be.' Stacie was shaking her head again. 'But how can I leave Mum and Danny?'

'It's such an amazing opportunity to go to Australia and try out a new life over there. I can't see your mum wanting to stand in your way.'

'That's the worst part, she wouldn't want to do that in a million years, but how can I just leave her to cope with caring for Danny on her own? My stepfather is worse than useless and he hasn't sent any money for Danny for years. Without my wages, Mum and Danny would have far less time together and far less spare cash to do anything fun. It wouldn't be fair of me just to go and if I'd thought there was any chance of me falling for Greg as hard as I have, I would never have gone out with him in the first place.'

'What about Greg? Would he consider looking for a job over here, instead?'

'I think he would, eventually. But his dad has Parkinson's disease and it's deteriorated in recent years, so I think Greg feels the pull of being at home in Australia and close to his parents just as strongly as I do being here for Mum and Danny.'

Claudia didn't say anything for a moment, as Jennie finally arrived back at their table with the two coffees, and she was far less confident than she had been that she could say anything of use. Stacie and Greg were being pulled in opposite directions and both of them had such strong reasons to hold firm that there didn't seem to be a way it could be resolved. Well certainly not one Claudia could come up with immediately. If only it were as easy as writing a prescription.

'Can you carry on with the relationship on a long-distance basis, do you think?'

'I guess we could, but we're talking about the other side of the world, here. He couldn't be any further away if he tried!'

'So what are you going to do?

'I've got two choices. I can either say nothing to Mum and say goodbye to Greg in a couple of weeks, knowing there's a good chance I'll never see him again.' Stacie sighed. 'Or I can talk to the one person I should talk to about this sort of decision — my mum — and see what she thinks I should do. I just don't know if I can put that burden on her.'

'I know I've only met Nicola once, but I do think she'd want to know.' Claudia paused and took a sip of her coffee, wondering if she really should be giving this sort of advice to someone she'd known for such a short time. 'I just don't think she'll ever forgive herself if she finds out later and realises you didn't feel able to talk it through with her.'

'I know and that's why I've decided that I've got to find a way of telling her about the proposal, but I need to make it clear that I haven't made up my mind to say yes, even though Greg insisted I had to hold on to the ring in the meantime.' She twisted the band nervously on her finger. 'I suppose now's as good a time as any.' Draining her coffee, Stacie got to her feet.

'Just phone me if you need anything.' Claudia gave what she hoped was a reassuring smile, but she didn't miss the heaviness of her friend's steps as she walked out of the pub. Knowing only too well how it felt to disappoint her own mother, she didn't envy Stacie the conversation she was about to have. It was obvious Nicola loved Stacie though, so they'd find a way to work it out together. Sadly, Claudia had never had that sort of confidence in her relationship with her own mother and, despite Stacie's current dilemma, that was something she *did* envy.

* * *

Finally curling up on her bed watching the documentary on Alaska, after finishing the takeaway she'd had delivered, it wasn't long before Claudia drifted off to sleep. Waking with a start at the sound of the phone ringing, she glanced at the clock on her bedside table; it was nine pm.

'Hello,' she croaked into the phone.

'Sorry darling, did I wake you?' A gentle male voice gradually filtered through Claudia's fuddled head.

'Hello, Dad.' She pulled herself upright. 'I wasn't asleep,' she lied, not wanting him to worry that he might have disturbed her. 'How are you?'

'Not so bad.' It was her dad's turn to lie. Claudia could have sworn that since that last fateful row with her mother, when she'd decided she had to get out of Manchester and as far away from her as possible, that even had father's voice had changed. She'd left him to deal with Juliet alone and be the focus of all her attention and the criticism that came with it; no wonder he sounded worn out.

'What have you been up to?' she asked, hoping he'd say he'd been doing something other than throwing himself into work or answering to his wife's every beck and call.

'I've started playing golf again.' He was almost whispering now and she wondered if her mother was at home with him or maybe even listening in to the call. She didn't think he'd do that to her, but then again he'd never been able to stand up to his wife in the way that he should. 'Your mum said it might help me make some useful connections, next time I want to go for a promotion.' He sounded as though he was trying to convince himself. He'd told Claudia more than once that he'd wanted to train to be a GP when he'd first qualified as a doctor, but it was Juliet who'd persuaded him that a hospital career was a better option and he was now a consultant. Only it wasn't what her father had wanted, it was Juliet's decision — just like everything in their family life had always been.

'Well at least it gets you out of the house.' Even if her mother was listening in, she wasn't pulling any punches. After the last row they'd had, it was hardly worth pretending that they saw eye to eye anymore.

'Well, there is that.' Her dad laughed,

confirmation that her mother wasn't within earshot. 'What about you, are you making the most of living your own life, now that you've escaped?'

'You could escape too, you know.'

'It's different for me. I knew exactly what I was getting into when I married your mother, I chose this life.' He sounded as though he couldn't quite believe it himself. 'You on the other hand were born into it, you didn't have a choice.'

'I still can't understand how, after you'd been brought up by someone as loving as Grandma, that you'd choose someone like Mum.'

'I've told you before, she was beautiful and brilliant. I was bowled over by her. I know she can be forceful, but she only wants what's best for us.'

'You mean what *she* thinks is best for us and I think controlling is a more accurate description than forceful.' Claudia had been the dutiful daughter and completed her medical training. There'd never been any question that she'd follow her parents into medicine, it was her passion and she was grateful that they'd instilled that in her. But, like her father before her, she'd always wanted to be a GP and no amount of pushing, sulking or emotional blackmail from her mother had managed to change her mind. Maybe they were actually more alike than she thought, she could be pretty stubborn too when she put her mind to it. That final row, though, when her mother had turned up at the surgery she was working in, near the hospital where Juliet worked as a consultant psychiatrist, had been the last straw. Her mother had told her that she was wasting her life and that being a GP was nothing more than acting as a gatekeeper for *real medicine*, as she put it. She'd accused her daughter of plumping for the safe and boring option and Claudia had been determined to prove her wrong. The job in St. Finbar's Cross was a locum role she took to get her out of Manchester as soon as she could, but she wanted to be a general practitioner somewhere that would challenge her and prove to her mother that it wasn't always the safe option. So she'd set her heart on securing a role in Alaska, or failing that somewhere tropical, maybe with an organisation like *Médecins Sans Frontières*, or as a volunteer in the developing world. General practice didn't have to mean routine.

'But you like it there?' Her father clearly needed reassurance that she was okay. He was probably the only thing she missed about not living in Manchester any more.

'I love it.' The words surprised Claudia, she hadn't realised how much she'd come to enjoy life in St. Finbar's Cross, and so quickly too.

'Is there any chance you might decide to hang around?' Her father sounded much older all of a sudden. 'At least I can hop in the car and come down to see you in Devon. If you go to Alaska, I'll never get to see you.'

'You could always come for a holiday.' She didn't add that her mother wouldn't be invited, some things didn't need any explanation.

'And you could come home before you head off overseas. Promise me you'll try to clear the air with your mother before you go, otherwise I'm terrified you might never come back.'

'Okay, Dad. I promise to try, but I'm not going to change my mind about my career plans, so I wouldn't hold your breath about Mum and I being able to be in the same room without having a row.'

'I know, love, and I'm not asking you to change, all I'm asking is that you give your mum one last chance to change.'

'If that's what you want, Dad. I'm doing it for you though.'

'I know, darling, and I love you all the more for that.'

'I love you too, Dad.'

Replacing the receiver, she hoped she could find the strength to keep the promise she'd just made, but the thought of seeing her mum again — and hearing the same old disappointment in her voice — filled Claudia with dread.

5

By the following Friday, Stacie had confided in Claudia that she still hadn't been able to speak to her mother about Greg's proposal. When she'd got home, that night after telling Claudia everything in the pub, she'd discovered that Danny had picked up an infection and her mother was already under pressure as a result. She hidden the engagement and told Claudia that she was still waiting for the right time, but it was hard to envisage when that might be.

'I don't know what to say.' Stacie gave a small shrug of her shoulders as she spoke. 'Telling two of the people that you love most in the world that a big part of you wants to leave them to be with someone else is hard enough. But with Mum having Danny to worry about all the time, I just don't want to add to her stress.'

Despite her friend's reservations, Claudia was sure Nicola would want the best for Stacie, no matter what personal cost that had for her. Funny how some people just seemed cut out to be maternal and others seemed to have that part of them missing, even when they'd raised a family. It had worried Claudia from time to time that, if she ever had children of her own, she might turn out like her mother. That was a sobering thought.

'What are you two whispering about?' Claudia jumped as she heard Theo's voice behind them and Stacie dropped the red pen, which she'd been doodling the word *Australia* with on a scrap of paper.

'Nothing.' Claudia turned towards him and Stacie screwed the piece of paper up, before busying herself with the morning's post.

'Well it all looks suspicious.' Theo looked tired, as if the weekend couldn't come too soon for him. 'You aren't up to something are you? Organising a surprise birthday party or planning to redecorate the surgery so it looks like Stacie's car?' Stacie had flower stickers all over her car and the front headlights even had eyelashes. No wonder he was worried about a surgery make-over. Theo grinned and immediately looked far less worn out than he had a moment before.

'Oh no!' Claudia slapped the palm of her hand against her forehead, feigning distress. 'We had no idea your birthday was coming up, it's a big one too, I'll bet? After all, it's not every year that you hit forty!' Claudia laughed at the expression on his face. She knew full well that he wasn't celebrating a 'big' birthday, but she liked the way they were comfortable enough to tease each other about things. It wasn't something she'd experienced with her colleagues much before. That was probably down to her, though. She'd never had a sibling to play-fight with and her mother thought jokes were a waste of time, so she'd probably given her ex-colleagues that impression too.

'Not every year, you're right,' he agreed. 'And not for another five years in my case. Just for that, I'm not going to let you off the hook for any longer. My sister Janey has been on at me again about sorting out this lunch date. How about tomorrow, have you got any plans?'

'No, nothing I can't put on hold.' She'd seen a vacancy advertised in the States that she was interested in applying for, but she needed to spend some time researching visa issues and that sort of thing. It was something she was planning to do over the weekend. If everything worked out, her days in St. Finbar's Cross could soon be numbered and with becoming Stacie's only confidant, and the deepening of her friendships with her other colleagues at the surgery, it was starting to feel like more of wrench than she'd ever imagined it would — which was all the more reason to leave sooner rather than later.

'That's settled then. I'll pick you up just before twelve and that will get Janey off my back too.' Theo smiled again. 'I do wonder if she'll ever stop being the big sister and bossing me around.'

'Sounds like she knows how to keep you in your place.' Claudia returned his smile, but there was that sense of emptiness again that she so often felt when she heard about other people's families. She'd have loved a sibling, someone with whom she could share the burden of her relationship with her mother, someone who really understood what it felt like to be the child of someone so intense. As it was, the only person she'd felt able to turn to, her grandmother, was now gone. Her dad meant well and she knew he loved her, but he'd spent so long dancing to her mother's tune that he couldn't seem to break the habit. That's why Claudia's only chance to break the cycle was to move away, even if that meant leaving behind a place she could easily learn to love. St. Finbar's Cross was beginning to weave its magic, so she couldn't afford to wait too much longer.

* * *

'Wow!' Claudia hadn't taken the valley road out of St. Finbar's Cross before and had never seen the beautiful thatched cottage, which looked as though it belonged on the cover of a chocolate box.

'It's stunning isn't it?' Theo sounded wistful, as the car slowed to a stop. 'It's taken a lot of work, especially since my brother-in-law's accident and with the house being Grade II listed, but somehow they managed to do it.' Theo's voice trailed off and Claudia squeezed his hand. He'd told her about the skiing accident his brother-in-law, Sean, had suffered. Paralysed from the waist down as a result, it sounded like he and Janey had been to hell and back. Theo had said it had made him and his sister closer and he'd taken care of

Sean's medical issues whenever he could, to try and keep life as normal as possible. There were things to think about that other people weren't aware of when they saw someone in a wheelchair. Everything from catheters to avoiding the results of too much pressure causing issues with his legs. According to Theo, Sean hated all of that — anything that made him feel different — so Theo worked with him to keep as much of it under wraps as they could, from the children in particular, and it sounded as though not much held Sean back.

'Come on then, let's get you in there. Although I warn you that the Spanish Inquisition has nothing on Janey and she's determined to see me settle down again before I hit that big Four O you mentioned earlier.' Theo pulled a face. 'So try not to read too much into it, if she starts to intimate that we might become more than just friends.'

'I won't.' She wanted to reassure him that she knew only too well about family members who wanted to force their own agenda on you, but talking about her mother would immediately bring down her day and she didn't want to do that.

* * *

Stepping inside Sean and Janey's house was like a breath of fresh air. It was a guaranteed mood lifter too. Everywhere around them were brightly coloured children's paintings. Two young children rushed out of the lounge and swooped on Theo, before he even had a chance to finish introducing Claudia and Janey.

'Uncle Theo, look what I made. A dinosaur!' A little girl of about six thrust a model made from egg boxes into Theo's arms.

'Wow!' He looked suitably impressed. 'Is it a Stegosaurus?' He examined the haphazardly constructed egg boxes carefully, as though they were an infinitely precious fossil.

'No, silly!' The little girl stood in front

of him with her hands on her hips. 'It's a Tyrannosaurus Rex, of course.' The expression on her face spoke a thousand words — adults could be so slow sometimes.

'Oh!' Theo whacked his hand against his forehead. 'How could I be so stupid. I'm sorry Laura, it's so obviously a Tyrannosaurus Rex, I don't know what I was thinking!' He smiled conspiratorially at Claudia, but Laura's brother couldn't keep quiet.

'It's just a load of egg boxes, that's why Uncle Theo couldn't tell. I'm Marcus and I'm eight.' As he spoke, he held out his hand to Claudia, as if he were more like *twenty*-eight. Even as he shook Claudia's hand, Laura was already pinching his arm, in the wonderful way that brothers and sisters of that age so often do.

'It looked a lot better until you sat on it you big pig!' Laura was indignant and as Marcus tugged on one of her plaits, things started to turn nasty.

'I'd better sort these two out.' Janey

looked over the top of the squabbling children's heads at Claudia and Theo. 'You two go through to Sean, he's waiting for you.'

★ ★ ★

'Hello mate!' Sean greeted Theo warmly as they entered the sitting room. Even though he was confined to a wheelchair, it was obvious to Claudia that he worked hard to stay fit and he looked as though he might jump up from the chair at any minute and go back to the life that Theo said he'd had before. He'd been planning on opening an adventure centre just before his accident and had the sort of complexion that looked as though he spent every spare minute outdoors.

'You must be Claudia?' Sean gave her a quick, appraising stare and turned to wink at Theo. 'You're right. She is gorgeous. No wonder he's been hiding you up at the medical centre for so long.' When he laughed, Sean looked like a schoolboy and the twinkle in his eye hadn't been extinguished by his accident.

'I don't think Theo wanted to spend part of his weekend with me, as well as all week at work.' Even as she spoke, Claudia knew that wasn't true. Try as she might to deny it, there was a chemistry between her and Theo, which neither of them could take any further. All the same, it was clear that Sean had been briefed by Janey and the attempts at match-making were anything but subtle.

'That's where you're wrong, in fact Theo told me that . . . ' Sean was cut off in mid-flow, as Theo clamped a hand over his brother-in-law's mouth.

'I think you've said enough.' He was smiling as he spoke. 'Who said that confiding in a friend was a good idea?'

Theo and Sean had the sort of relationship which could only have developed over years of friendship and Claudia soon found out that they'd first met at school, long before Sean started to date Theo's sister. By the time Janey came into the sitting room with some drinks and dips, they were already regaling Claudia with tales of their school days.

'We even got suspended once!' Sean's face was animated as he spoke. 'All we were doing was a good deed too.'

'Yes, we were definitely unfairly treated.' Theo grinned at Claudia. 'We decided to give the mice in the biology lab their freedom.' Claudia could tell from the suppressed laughter in Theo's voice that there was more to the story.

'Tell Claudia exactly where you decided to free the poor things,' Janey interrupted their conversation, with a tone of voice that she probably used for the children when they were misbehaving.

'We thought it would be a good idea to keep them somewhere warm.' Sean gave Claudia a wide-eyed, innocent look.

'Where?' Claudia had already guessed that they hadn't put the mice, Blue-Peter-style, into a nice, safe, insulated box.

'We put them in gym bags, they were

warm and lined with PE kits.' Sean still had a look of total innocence on his face.

'Tell Claudia whose bags they were.' Janey was smiling too, even though she must have heard the story several times over the years.

'They were in the girls' changing room.' Theo tried to look apologetic. 'We knew the mice would be okay, we only slipped them in the bags a few minutes before the girls were going to get changed for PE.' Both men started to laugh.

'We could hear the girls' screaming from the playground,' Sean managed to say between bursts of laughter and Claudia found it easy to imagine him and Theo as schoolboys.

'Sad isn't it?' Janey turned to her with a rueful smile. 'Still, boys will be boys.'

'How do you put up with them? Look, he's corrupting your children now!' Claudia gestured towards Theo, who was showing Laura and Marcus how to jam a breadstick sideways into their mouths.

'I know.' Janey was still smiling. 'But what can you do when you love them?'

Claudia nodded, not trusting herself to speak. There was that pang again. She knew exactly what Theo's sister meant and the time she spent with her grandmother as a child had given her that same sense of family and feeling of warmth. What scared her was that she might never be able to replicate it with a family of her own. She wanted to stay in Sean and Janey's house forever, and their family was one more thing to love about St. Finbar's Cross.

'Would you like to see the rest of the house?' Janey's voice interrupted her thoughts and she nodded, grateful for the distraction. 'Be careful as you come up the stairs, it's a bit narrower than it used to be.' Theo's sister led the way and Claudia soon realised what she meant. A stair-lift took up a considerable amount of the cottage's stairwell.

'Theo organised it.' The gratitude in

Janey's voice was audible. 'Sean didn't want to move our bedroom downstairs, he likes to keep things normal.'

'It must have been difficult.' Claudia wanted to kick herself. Why couldn't you ever find something profound or even useful to say in these sort of situations? The family seemed to have taken Sean's accident in their stride.

'It was really hard at first, but Sean's still Sean.' Janey gave her a warm smile. 'And Theo's been fantastic, with his help Sean was able to come home from rehab a lot sooner than originally planned and it's at least partly because of him that Sean is now cooking up plans again to open up his adventure centre, but this time to help others who've had spinal injuries to get involved in exciting activities.'

Janey showed Claudia around the children's rooms and she was stunned by the wonderful murals that Sean had painted on their bedroom walls before his illness. In Janey and Sean's room was an antique bookcase that stretched floor to ceiling, lined with hundreds of different books. Janey carefully selected one, then drew it out to show her. It was a children's book, beautifully illustrated with fairies and goblins dancing across the cover.

'Sean did it.' Janey pointed to the front cover of the book which bore Sean's name as the illustrator.

'They're beautiful.' Claudia turned it over in her hand and looked at the illustrations carefully. 'Aren't those the children's faces?' She could see that one of the fairies had been based on Laura and the biggest of the goblins looked just like Marcus.

'He always puts us or people he knows into his drawings.' Janey smiled and pulled another book from the shelf. 'This one's called *The Enchanted Princess*.'

On the cover of the book was a beautiful woman, dressed in a Cinderella-style gown with her long dark hair swept up into a glittering crown. Despite the fact that Janey was dressed in jeans and a sweatshirt, the woman on the cover of the book was undeniably her.

'He always calls me princess, so it just seemed appropriate.' Tears glistened in Janey's eyes. 'It's been five years since his accident and he only re-discovered his love for drawing in the weeks and months after his accident, when he had so much time on his hands and he was going stir-crazy in the hospital. It was Theo who reminded him how much he'd always loved art at school. The hospital had an art therapist and they put on an exhibition. Sean's work got a lot of attention and it was spotted by a local writer, who wanted to pitch some ideas to a publisher and was looking for an illustrator to work with. It's led to a whole new career and it's just another thing we've got Theo to thank for. Annoying as younger brothers so often are, I wouldn't swap mine for the world.'

'I can tell he feels the same way about you.' Claudia was feeling more and more drawn to Theo. She'd been hoping that meeting his family might actually help to dampen the feelings she hadn't wanted to develop for him, but it was having the opposite effect.

⋆ ⋆ ⋆

By the time Theo drove them away from the house, several hours later, Claudia felt as though she'd known Sean and Janey Sullivan for years. Despite everything the couple had been through, they were as warm and welcoming as anyone Claudia had ever known. The Sullivan house was full of laughter and the children were a delight, even when they were bickering with each other which they frequently had, even in the few hours that she'd spent with them.

'They're lovely,' Claudia spoke as Theo's Land Rover sped through the dark back towards the centre of the village.

'Well, obviously I think so, but I'm

very glad to hear that you do too.'

'Your sister couldn't say enough about what you've done to help them.'

'It was nothing. It's just what family does isn't it?' Theo kept his eyes on the road and she was glad he couldn't look at her as a result.

'Some families.' Claudia suddenly wanted to let him know about her family life. It was the reason she wouldn't be hanging around it St. Finbar's Cross and the more she got to know Theo, the more she felt he had a right to know the truth. 'My mother is what you might call an *interesting* character. It's always been her way or the highway and so I never had the sort of life growing up that Marcus and Laura do. I had my grandmother though and thank goodness she gave me a taste of what family life should be all about.'

'I did wonder why you never mention your family.'

'My dad's a hospital consultant who'd be much happier as a country

GP somewhere like this, but that would never had been enough for Mum. She's a consultant psychiatrist and she'd dragged him all over the country chasing promotion after promotion for one or other of them. They've been in Manchester for quite a while now, though. She thinks my desire to be a GP equals boredom, so I promised myself I'd prove her wrong and find somewhere to practise that's anywhere but boring. We had a huge row, so I had to get as far away from her as possible for a bit, which is how I ended up doing locum work, but I really want to work somewhere different, like Alaska or another challenging area to practise in. Who knows, maybe I'll even end up as a flying doctor in the Outback or something.'

'Is that what *you* want though? Or would you be happy to settle down somewhere like this?' There was a note of hope in his voice that she couldn't bear to destroy completely. Truth she'd forgotten a long time ago what she really wanted. She'd become obsessed with proving her mother wrong and, until she did that, she could never live the life she really wanted even if she found it along the way.

'Do you fancy a drink?' Claudia broke the silence as Theo drew up outside the Golden Fleece Hotel. Against her better judgement, she really wanted to spend some more time with him.

'I thought you'd never ask!' Theo smiled at last and turning towards her, he kissed her gently before pulling away. 'In case I forget to tell you later. Thanks for tonight.'

She was glad of the darkness as she stepped out of the Land Rover. This was a dangerous game she was playing, toying with both of their emotions and she had a horrible feeling that neither of them would escape without being hurt. Theo could end up as just one more victim of her mother's vicious tongue, even if he never met her.

*　*　*

'You never answered my question.' Theo brought their drinks over to the table. 'Can you really not see yourself living and working permanently somewhere like this?'

'I love being a GP and I think I *could* do that anywhere, but that doesn't mean I want to stay in the first place that feels comfortable. I'm sure that Sean would agree with me that comfortable is the easy option, but sometimes we need to keep challenging ourselves. He's not showing any sign of deviating from his ambitions, so what excuse have I got?' Theo had made her think though. Were those really *her* ambitions or just the ammunition she'd developed to counter her mother's arguments?

'I'm not so sure Sean would agree with you, at least not if he knows what's good for him.' Theo offered her another one of his disarming smiles. 'You seem at home here. I haven't enjoyed working with a series of locums since my partner in the practice retired, but St. Finbar's

Cross isn't the sort of place that everyone could make their home, so I need to make sure that any permanent replacement is the right fit. For all of us.' As Theo spoke, Claudia looked around at the crowded pub.

'Plenty of people seem to love it here.' She gestured towards the groups of people clustered around the tables to the right of them. There were several young lads who looked as though they might work on one of the local farms, and the other table was occupied by a family group, who encompassed at least four generations.

'I suppose if working here isn't enough, you'd need another reason to stay.' As Theo spoke their eyes met briefly. 'Although even that's not enough for some people.' He sounded very matter of fact, but Claudia would have bet a month's salary that he was referring to his ex-wife.

'What was her name?' Stacie had told her a bit about Theo's ex-wife, but she didn't want him to think they'd been gossiping behind his back. In any case, she wanted to hear about her from him — this woman who could walk away from Theo Harrison without a backward glance? Claudia was already beginning to realise it wouldn't be that easy for her.

'Sara Johnson.' Theo smiled at her. 'If you mean my ex-wife? I should have guessed she'd never settle for life here when she didn't even want to become a Harrison by taking my name when we got married. It was like she already had an escape route planned. I'm sure you've heard a bit about it?'

'I knew you were divorced, but not a lot else.' Claudia felt uncomfortable, questioning him about a painful part of his past; she still wanted to hear it, if he was willing to tell her.

'It's okay.' Theo laughed, clearly amused. 'I'm not tortured by it, the way some people round here might have you believe. In fact, it was a joint decision in the end.'

'Really?' She wasn't sure why she felt

quite so relieved that he wasn't still pining away for a lost love.

'Sara was a solicitor. We originally met just after university but, when I came back to St. Finbar's Cross to set up the practice, she just couldn't settle.' Theo took a sip of his drink. 'I was happy to be home, but Sara said she felt like she was in a goldfish bowl. Everywhere we went, I knew someone. You know how the locals are, they love a chat and I think it's all part of the charm of village life. Anyway, Sara wanted to practise law in London and she even wangled me an interview with one of the hospitals there.' Theo sighed. 'The trouble is she planned it all without telling me, sent off an application to the hospital and even put a deposit on a flat. At that stage I hadn't even agreed to *think* about leaving St. Finbar's Cross.'

'You're joking!' She was all for going after what you wanted but Sara's actions seemed a bit extreme. Theo's ex sounded like she'd get on really well with Claudia's mother; neither woman seemed likely to let a little thing — like someone else's point of view — stand in the way of what *they* wanted.

'No, it's all true.' Theo was smiling again. 'I think that signalled the beginning of the end. Sara didn't want to stay in St. Finbar's Cross and I didn't want to be forced into moving to the city. So that was that, no dramatic broken hearts or anything exciting. Unfortunately, I think local legend has it that I'm now a shadow of my former self.' Theo fixed her with a serious look for once. 'But I can assure you that I'm happier than I've ever been and if I let someone into my life now it would be for all the right reasons.'

'That's a pretty good place to be in your life.' Claudia swallowed, wishing she could be as sure that she was on the right path.

'The funny thing is that Sean always knew Sara wasn't *The One*, as he calls it.' Theo screwed his face up slightly as he spoke. 'He always was a know-it-all, and I guess he'd seen me date enough girls over the years to work out when it wasn't going to last. Sean said he knew without a doubt that Janey was the one for him. I guess he just wanted me to have what they've got. I should have listened to him and Janey when they told me I shouldn't rush into marrying Sara, but I can't have my big sister running my life forever.'

'Have he and Janey been together since you were kids?' As Claudia asked the question, Theo smiled at the memory.

'No, she's only two years older than us, but it seemed like a gap of light years when we were young. She was off at university and then working for an advertising agency in Paris for while, whilst I was studying. She and Sean both happened to visit me during the same weekend, when I was doing my pre-registration year at Muirsfield Hospital. A lot had changed and that two year gap suddenly meant nothing. When they saw each other again, it was bam! Love at *second* sight.'

'And I suppose you had no part in engineering their being with you at the same time?' Claudia lowered her gaze as she spoke and swirled the glass from side to side. It must be nice for Janey to have a brother like Theo, someone who was always looking out for you.

'As if I'd do something like that!' There was a twinkle in his eye that completely gave the game away. No wonder Sean was so desperate for this brother-in-law and best friend to find his own love story.

'Maybe he'll return the favour and put in a good word for you, next time you meet someone you really like.'

'I'm banking on it.' Theo shot her a look that left her in no doubt he was talking about her. If only she'd been planning to stay, there might have been something between them. But, as it was, their fate was already sealed.

6

True to the promise he'd made, Theo agreed to give Claudia the riding lesson that she'd made a donation to the auction of promises for, on a crisp Saturday afternoon in October. He lived in a beautiful sandstone cottage in a lane off the road that led out of town towards Janey and Sean's place. The front garden was a riot of autumn colour, as the winds had been fairly light and the leaves still clung steadfastly to the trees that towered above the quintessential Devonshire cottage, with its thatched roof and leaded windows. Inside it had a more modern, minimalist looked. The beams had been sandblasted back to the original wood and the décor was what she might have expected from a busy man living on his own. The lounge was dominated by two huge leather sofas and not much else.

There was no clutter of ornaments around the place and only a few pictures hung on the walls, although Claudia noticed one of Sean's illustrations amongst them.

'Are you ready to hit the bridle paths then? There's some beautiful countryside around here. So even if my riding tuition isn't up to much, you should still enjoy it.' Theo gestured out of the window to the field behind the cottage. Two horses grazed lazily, flicking their tails to ward off the few remaining insects which hadn't completely disappeared for winter.

'I haven't been on a horse in years.' For a moment, Claudia couldn't remember the last time she'd been on a horse and then it came back to her. 'It was in Wales, it must have been at least twenty years ago. Nan booked up a pony trekking holiday, but I ended up falling off more often than I managed to trek anywhere very much. Even my grandmother, who was well over seventy by then, was far better at it than me.' She laughed at the memory, despite being almost able to feel the bruises that had sprung up all over her during the week's pony trekking.

'Mable will look after you. She's the smaller of the two.' Claudia followed Theo's gaze to a chestnut mare that, even to her untrained eye, looked quite elderly. 'I've had her since I was fifteen and she's twenty three now. We call her *Mable, Slow and Stable*, she's really very safe.'

'Are you sure it's not going to be too much for her, having to cart around an absolute novice like me, at her age?'

'Come on, you'll enjoy it, I promise.' Theo paused for a moment when Claudia hesitated, but then he grinned. 'You can trust me you know, I'm a doctor.'

* * *

Once they were outside, Theo moved quickly. He removed the horses' rugs and began saddling them up as deftly as

107

he might have examined one of his patients. He was clearly an expert, which did nothing at all to calm Claudia's nerves.

'What's your horse called?' Claudia asked, as Theo did up the girth of the bigger horse's saddle. It was half again as big as Mable and such a dark bay colour that it almost looked black.

'Fire.' Theo's voice was muffled as he answered, his face obscured as he ran his hand down the horse's legs, checking for lumps and bumps.

'Oh, I see.' Claudia raised her eyebrows. 'So I get the ancient Mable, Slow and Stable and you get Fire, a body double for Black Beauty if ever I saw one!'

At that moment, Fire lost his patience, let out a high whinny and kicked sideways with his back legs. Luckily Theo was far too quick for the horse and he directed another of his disarming smiles at Claudia. 'Well you could always ride Fire if you like.' Having jumped back about twenty paces when the horse had kicked out, she said nothing but shook her head vigorously in response.

He gave her a leg up into the saddle and she was relieved straight away to realise that he'd been telling the truth. Mable was nothing if not safe, in fact Claudia had to squeeze the old mare's sides with all her strength to get the horse to move at all. Eventually, the four of them set off across the fields at the back of Theo's house and headed up towards the landmark that gave St. Finbar's Cross its name.

'Are you sure you don't want to swap?' Theo pulled Fire to a halt as he spoke, giving Claudia and Mable a chance to catch up. The old horse wasn't the only one out of breath by the time they drew level with Theo.

'I feel like I've carried Mable up the hill rather than the other way round!' Her cheeks were flushed with warmth and her blonde hair was escaping from the riding hat he'd lent her. She must have looked like she'd been dragged through a hedge backwards, but each time she looked up, Theo was watching her with a smile on his face.

'Perhaps we should take it a bit more gently? Mable hasn't been ridden for a while and you look a bit worn out too.'

'Are you saying that us girls can't handle it?' Claudia leant down and patted Mable affectionately. 'Just because we're both a bit out of practice.'

'See, this is just another benefit that life in the country could bring you. Regular opportunities to go riding.' Theo was less than subtle about dropping the sort of hints that might have persuaded her to stay in different circumstances. Despite how torn it was starting to make her feel, she was secretly pleased to know that he liked having her around.

'Plenty of practise for when I have to ride through the Outback on my rounds then.'

'Let's go up to the cross.' Theo adjusted the peak of his riding hat. 'And if the view from up there doesn't convince you that we've got more to offer than the Australian bush, then nothing will.'

* ★ ★

Despite Claudia's protests that she and Mable could keep up the pace, she was glad when Theo slowed down and the four of them made their way leisurely to the top of the hill. St. Finbar's Cross itself was fenced off, but the view from the gateway, where they stopped, was spectacular. The village sprawled out below them and Claudia could easily make out Theo's house, the medical centre and The Golden Fleece Hotel. Strange, but this funny little place was already starting to feel so familiar. Maybe that was what happened when you've never really felt at home anywhere, it was easy to feel content wherever you went. At least that was what Claudia tried to convince herself.

'My grandmother would have loved this.' To her surprise, Claudia could mention her without feeling sad. 'She was always really fond of the West Country and I think she'd have moved down this way if she hadn't needed to stay closer to Manchester for me. Her house was always my bolt hole when life with mum got just that bit too intense.'

'There's nowhere else in the world I'd rather live, that's for sure. Shall we go back down and look at the village from closer quarters?' Theo urged Fire forwards as he spoke and the horse responded instantly. Getting Mable moving again was going to be more of a challenge though.

They made their way down the hill and into the village. As they got closer to Theo's house, Mable suddenly broke into an unsteady canter, something Claudia hadn't even thought the horse was capable of.

'Whoah!' She tried in vain to pull on the reins, but when the old mare made up her mind she could be very determined.

'Are you okay?' Theo called out, pushing Fire into a canter and catching up with Mable almost immediately

'I think so.' Her voice wobbled, a

repeat of the bruises she'd sustained on that pony trekking holiday seemed inevitable. 'Only I think Mable's brakes seem to have failed!'

'She knows she's close to the feed shed, that's the problem.' As Theo spoke, he moved past her. Bringing Fire to an abrupt halt, he managed to block Mable's path. The old mare shuddered to an undignified stop and Claudia shot halfway up the horse's neck, before thudding back down into the saddle.

'Well that took me by surprise.' She patted Mable's neck, strangely pleased that her elderly mount still had some fighting spirit.

'Are you okay to carry on or would you rather go back to the cottage?' The worried expression on Theo's face melted away as she started to laugh.

'I'm fine honestly.' She patted Mable's neck again. 'It was actually quite exciting in a terrifying kind of way. I suppose Mable's more like me than I thought, far too keen on her food!'

* ★ ★

Having survived Mable's decision to bolt, it was a relief that she seemed happy to return to her usual plodding pace as they rode through the village. Losing control of the horse in the middle of St. Finbar's Cross, with half her patients likely to cross their path at any moment, was an embarrassment Claudia could happily live without.

'Isn't that Mrs Jessop?' She felt confident enough to let go of the reins with one hand and point over towards a garden, where the surgery's most cantankerous patient was busy weeding.

Theo nodded and urging Fire on into a trot, he drew level with Mrs Jessop's gate, Mable following in half-hearted pursuit.

'Hello there Mrs Jessop!' Theo called out as the old lady looked up from her position seated on a gardening stool.

'You almost had me over, Doctor. I didn't expect to find a huge, snorting horse leaning over my garden gate.' Mrs

Jessop tutted loudly. 'Whatever are you doing, trying to give me a heart attack? I've read about how easily they're caused you know and . . . .' Mrs Jessop was in full flow, but Theo managed to cut her off.

'I was just admiring your gardening stool.' He gestured towards the low seat from which Mrs Jessop was reaching down to do her weeding. 'I'm so glad that you decided to take Dr Taylor's advice and get something to help you with the Baker's cyst.'

'I was going to buy a stool anyway.' Mrs Jessop gave a snort, as if her trip to the surgery had been nothing more than the waste of time she'd said it was.

'And what about the befriending service, have you contacted them?' Claudia addressed the older woman, who didn't seem willing to look her in the eye. Still, Mrs Jessop didn't really stand a chance of intimidating her, she spent a life time with a mother who could run rings around any awkward patient she might encounter.

'They're sending someone round.' Mrs Jessop gave another snort that would give Fire a run for his money. 'I just hope it's someone who's handy around the garden. I haven't got time to just sit around supping tea and making small talk.'

Despite her barbed words, Claudia couldn't resist smiling. Mrs Jessop might never admit it, but the suggestions she and Theo had made, and which their patient had reluctantly followed, could make a change to her life for the better. So it might not be the sort of life saving surgery her mother would like to have seen her performing, but it was more than enough to give Claudia a warm glow.

'I'm sure the befriender they send you will be delighted to help you out.' Theo's eyes met Claudia's as he spoke and they exchanged a look of complete understanding.

'Well like I said, I haven't got time for idle chit chat.' The old lady turned her back on them and returned to the weeding. Without looking up she added, 'Goodbye Doctors, some of us have work to do you know.'

Leaving their ungrateful patient behind them, they made their way back through the village to Theo's cottage. It had been a perfect afternoon when for once everything seemed right in the world; but like day of endless blue sky, the threatening rain clouds were just over the horizon.

7

'What's wrong?' Claudia looked at her friend's tear-stained face as she entered the Golden Fleece Hotel. Stacie was perched on one of the sofas in the foyer looking like she was about to go in for root canal surgery. There was definitely something up.

'It's Greg, he's gone back to Australia.' The tears were flowing freely as she looked up at Claudia. 'I'm really sorry, I know I'm making a habit of coming to you with my problems, but I just don't have anyone else I feel like I can talk to at the moment.'

'I promise you, it's not a problem. Why don't we go up to my room and we can talk about it up there? It's a bit public here and I'm getting to know how much the locals like to gossip, so let's not make ourselves fodder for the next bulletin.' Claudia passed Stacie her key. 'You go up and make yourself comfortable and I'll bring us up some tea. Unless you fancy something stronger?'

'No, tea is good.' Stacie attempted a smile, but it turned into a sort of shuddering sigh instead. 'After all, tea is supposed to be able to cure all ills, isn't it?'

Whilst Claudia waited for the tea at the bar, all sorts of scenarios ran through her head. Maybe Greg had broken off the engagement because Stacie wasn't quick enough to tell the news to her family. It would be heartbreaking for Stacie if that was the case, but she'd probably had a lucky escape. After all, who wanted to love someone who didn't understand what made them tick, and only wanted life on their terms? Claudia could almost have laughed at the irony: she'd spent her whole life loving someone like that — even when she couldn't stand her mother, she still loved her and craved the approval that never came.

'Here we go. Hot tea and lots of sugar.' Claudia spoke as she pushed open the door to her room and set the tea tray out on the table in front of where Stacie was sitting, in one of the armchairs that flanked the fireplace.

'Thank you. Look, I'm sorry again about descending on you like this. You've probably got a million things to do, and the last thing you need is me turning up and telling you all my troubles.'

'Don't be silly. Just tell me whatever you feel comfortable talking about, or if you don't want to talk at all, we can just sit and drink tea instead. Believe me, I know what it's like not to have someone you feel you can turn to and I know you haven't been ready to talk to your mum yet.'

'That's just it! I was finally ready to speak to her, but I wanted to do it right. I've booked a day off from the surgery on Monday, because Danny has a teacher training day at school, and I wanted to take him and Mum out somewhere nice, somewhere I could talk to her about Greg and starting a new life in Australia. I can't seem to get it out when we're at home, and Danny is often hanging on our every word. By the time he's gone to bed, Mum's exhausted, and it's just not a conversation I feel I can start. I thought if we took him to the zoo or a play park or something, where he could be occupied, we could talk a bit more freely and I could stand a chance of not getting so emotional about it all.'

'That sounds like a really good plan.' Claudia smiled, recognising the need to try and take the emotion out of difficult conversations. 'Sometimes being out of your normal environment can help you to see things really clearly for the first time.'

'That's what I wanted for both of us, but now it suddenly seems out of my control again.' Fresh tears filled Stacie's eyes. 'Greg got a call from his mum to say his dad is having problems swallowing now, and the doctors don't seem completely sure if it's something they can treat, so Greg got on the first flight he could. Just in case . . . ' She wasn't quite able to finish the sentence.

'It must be so difficult for him, being so far away.'

'It's always going to be difficult for one of us, though, isn't it?'

'True, but, if you're meant to be together, I still think you can find a way to make it work.' Claudia's thoughts strayed briefly to Theo . . . but this wasn't about her, this was about Stacie and Greg.

'I hope so. We've already got so many plans. He wants to open his own hotel eventually, either in Australia, or back here in the West Country. He said he fell in love with it at the same time he fell in love with me.'

'And where would you rather be, if you didn't have all these complications pulling you both home?' Claudia had believed until recently that she *wanted* to escape somewhere exciting, but more and more she was starting to question what that could offer in comparison to what she would lose by leaving St. Finbar's Cross behind. Still she knew she had to go, even though she wasn't sure if it was what she wanted anymore.

'I think I'd still rather be here.'

'And what about Greg?'

'If he could bring his mum and dad with him, I think he'd want to be in England too. They're both from here originally anyway — they settled in Australia about ten years before Greg was born. They'd been told they couldn't have children and so they decided to go off and start a new life instead and opened a wildlife sanctuary out there. So it was one heck of a surprise when Greg arrived, because his mum was in her early forties and his dad was closer to fifty. I think, as an only child and with older parents, he's always been just as protective of them as they are of him.'

'He sounds like a good man.'

'He is.' Stacie managed a wry smile. 'Sometimes I almost wish he wasn't as wonderful as he is, it would make all of this so much easier for a start.'

'So how did you leave things?'

'Greg is going to see how his dad is, but if things don't settle down, he really wants me to go out there straight away so we can get married ... before anything happens that means his dad can't be there.' Stacie gave another long, shuddering sigh. 'But how can I just announce that to Mum? And I wouldn't want to get married without her there, it wouldn't even feel like I was if she wasn't there to witness it. Never mind starting a whole new life with her and Danny on the other side of the world. I just don't know if I can do it, but I can't bear the thought of losing Greg either.'

'Oh Stacie, I wish I could wave a magic wand to make everything right for you.'

'Just having you listen makes more difference than you could ever imagine.'

'The doctors over there might well be able to get things under control for

Greg's dad again, and take the pressure off you having to make such a huge decision so quickly.' Claudia caught Stacie's eye as she spoke, seeing the hope in her words reflected there. She only hoped she was right.

'It's what I'm praying for but, in the meantime, I owe it to Mum to be honest, even if leaving is something I'm only *thinking* about doing.'

'I'm sure you'll feel much better when you've spoken to your mum.' Claudia squeezed her friend's hand; it was a statement she'd never been able to make about her own life. But, either way, she trusted Stacie and Nicola to sort it out.

'Will you tell Theo what's going on for me? I want to be honest with him too. He's been a great boss, but more than that a good friend and I'd hate him to think I was hiding all this from him too, especially if I end up having to leave the surgery without working my notice.'

'Of course, I'll explain things to him

and I'm sure he'll understand too.' If Stacie left, Nicola wasn't the only one who'd miss her, but Claudia was beginning to realise that sometimes you had to stop caring what everyone else thought and do what was right for you. If only she could take her own advice.

8

Claudia could only imagine what Stacie was going through, building up the courage to tell her mum about her plans to start a new life on the other side of the world. She'd barely been able to sleep herself and, when she'd broken the news to Theo on the Sunday, she'd hardly known how to say it. The worst he was losing was an excellent receptionist and a good friend; Nicola and Danny stood to lose a whole lot more.

Typically, though, Theo had only been concerned about Stacie. He probably knew as well as anyone how hard a decision it was for her, and both of them were preoccupied with thoughts of how their friend was faring when they met up at the surgery on the Monday.

'I'm glad she's talking to her mum, anyway.' Theo smiled and Claudia felt her heavy heart lift a bit. He knew the family much better than she did and he didn't seem worried about how Nicola might take the news.

'Me too. I've been saying she should tell her mum since she told about Greg's proposal, but she was worried that, with Danny's cystic fibrosis and everything, it would pile too much pressure on.'

'If I know Nicola, she'll just want Stacie to be happy.' He paused and took a sip of his coffee. 'The family have been through lot, but Nicola's a bit like a lioness when it comes to her children. I've seen her go into battle with panels of medical professionals and the local authority to make sure Danny gets what he needs. All she'll want to do is protect Stacie and do everything in her power to make sure she gets what she really wants, even if it isn't something Nicola would choose.'

'It must be amazing to have a mother like that.' Claudia tried and failed to keep the wistful tone out of her voice. She was almost thirty; it was about time she came to terms with the idea that a loving mother was something she was never going to have. It had been worse since her grandmother's death. She'd always filled that void for Claudia, but now there was just Juliet with her sniping criticism. 'Sorry, I know it's not that long since you lost your mum.'

'That's okay. My parents were fantastic. I miss them, of course, but I know I'm lucky to have had a family life like that.' Theo smiled again, he was coming to understand her family issues, after the snippets of herself she'd gradually revealed in the weeks they'd known each other. In turn, he'd told her about losing his father when he was still at medical school and that his mother had died a year ago. He'd said it had made him and Janey closer than ever and that had been something else for Claudia to realise she'd never have. Envy was a futile emotion, but she couldn't help wishing again for that sibling she'd never have to talk about her mother with, maybe she could even have laughed with her brother or sister about some of her mother's antics then. As it was, laughter was about the last emotion her mother ever evoked in her.

★ ★ ★

Morning surgery was busy for Claudia and she didn't have too much time to dwell on worrying about Stacie or the fact that her feelings for Theo seemed to be shifting, beyond her will, into something more than friendship. Instead she concentrated on the job, thankful that the temporary receptionist had arrived and that the flow of patients had kept her mind occupied as a result. Just before lunchtime, Claudia had her last patient from the morning list.

'Good morning, Mr Forrester.' Claudia glanced down at the screen in front of her, again, as the patient entered the room to check when he'd last visited. 'How can I help you today?' She looked up and was face to face with a huge man in his late twenties. Kevin Forrester was built like a barn door. At about six feet four and around three hundred pounds, at a guess, he was quite an imposing sight. He seemed to fill half the room as he sat down opposite Claudia.

'It's my shoulder, Doctor. It's still giving me a lot of pain.' Kevin rotated his shoulder slightly and winced, as if to prove his point.

'The anti-inflammatory tablets you've been taking haven't had any effect then?' Claudia consulted his notes on the computer. Kevin had been suffering from a frozen shoulder for about six months and had been back and forth to the surgery for much of that time.

'It's getting stiffer, if anything.' He sighed deeply. 'And when I came to see the other doctor, he said I needed a steroid injection.' Kevin looked flushed all of a sudden and he shifted uncomfortably in the chair, which seemed much too small for him.

'Are you worried about taking steroids?' Claudia asked, aware that a lot of her patients had only heard about the negative effects of steroids when used in the wrong hands. 'The steroid injection is perfectly safe for this type of condition and won't result in the sort of side effects that you'd suffer if you were using steroids inappropriately.' Looking at Kevin, she doubted if he'd ever need to resort to steroids to build himself up.

'It's not the steroid part that worries me, Doctor.' As Kevin spoke, he didn't seem able to look her in the eyes. 'If truth be told, I'm petrified of injections!' He shuddered at just the mention of the word and Claudia suppressed a smile. Why was it that the most powerful of men could be turned into quivering wrecks by the prospect of an injection?

'Well, I could try to reassure you that the injection won't be all that painful.' She could tell by his expression that he was unlikely to be all that easily convinced. 'But, as you've been putting the injection off for nearly three months, according to your notes, I don't suppose that would get us very far.' Claudia kept her voice as gentle as she would have done if she had been speaking to a six-year-old who was afraid of injections. Although Kevin's fear was irrational, she was sympathetic enough to know that he couldn't control it and, in her experience, most people were capable of turning into six-year-olds if fear took hold.

'Isn't there any alternative to the injection?' His tone was almost desperate. 'I mean apart from these drugs, that is. They're just not working.'

'I can refer you to the hospital for treatment, although you might face a bit of a wait.' As Claudia spoke, Kevin's relief was tangible and he let out a long breath that he'd obviously been holding in. 'The hospital should be able to achieve the same results as the steroid injection by giving you ultrasound or laser treatment on your shoulder. They may even be able to offer you some physiotherapy to help with the condition.' She smiled warmly at Kevin, who looked like a reprieved prisoner at the prospect of avoiding the injection. 'The treatment won't work quite as quickly as the steroid injection would have done, but it should be just as effective in the long run.'

He leapt to his feet, leant across the desk and grasped Claudia by the shoulders, planting a wet kiss on her left cheek. The impromptu show of affection was all over before Claudia even had time to think about reaching for the panic button that was hidden under her desk.

'Thanks, Doctor, you're a marvel.' Kevin winked down at her from his great height. 'I don't suppose there's any chance that you'd let me buy you a drink in the Golden Fleece later?' He looked hopeful and, once again, Claudia forced herself to suppress a smile.

'Sorry, Mr Forrester.' She looked up at him, he seemed a different man already from the one who'd walked into her consulting room and she wanted to let him down easily. 'I'm afraid that wouldn't be appropriate. After all, I am your doctor and I find it's always best to keep that relationship strictly professional.'

'Whatever you say, Doc.' Kevin was still grinning. 'I knew you'd probably turn me down, but I had to try didn't I? Never mind, if you get my shoulder problem sorted out, I can get back in the pub darts team.' He winked at her again. 'There's always a good chance of meeting up in the pub once I'm playing regularly.' Kevin turned to leave, whistling to himself at the prospect of a return to form and no doubt at the thought of being able to lift a pint to his lips without wincing in pain.

Claudia was still smiling to herself as she typed up Kevin's notes and dictated a letter to the hospital referring him for treatment.

* * *

Just after twelve, Claudia switched off her Dictaphone and went through to the kitchen, which was empty. Even the table looked strangely bare, without the pile of doorstep sandwiches that Stacie usually insisted on making for everyone's lunch. Switching on the kettle, she spooned coffee into a mug; she didn't hear Theo come into the kitchen, so she jumped as he suddenly spoke.

'Had a good morning?' His tone was warm and he sounded as though he really wanted to know, rather than just making polite conversation.

'Busy, but good. What about you?' She turned to look at him as she spoke. 'Do you want a coffee?'

'Yes please to the coffee.' Theo took a seat at the table. 'My morning was pretty uneventful, until I got pulled into a half nelson by Kevin Forrester in reception. Even a frozen shoulder doesn't stop him confusing a show of affection with a rugby tackle.'

'I can imagine! What brought on the show of affection anyway?' Claudia passed him the coffee and sat down opposite Theo at the table.

'You.'

'Why would I make Kevin get you in a half nelson?'

'He wanted to tell me how brilliant you were and what a good job I'd done persuading someone like you to join the surgery at St. Finbar's Cross.' He smiled. 'Apparently you're a billion times better than the last locum we had.'

'Only a billion?' She couldn't resist smiling. Clearly turning down Kevin's offer of a drink hadn't done anything to dampen his good mood. 'I'll have to try harder.'

'I really wish you would think again about staying . . . long term.' Theo frowned slightly as he spoke and looking into his eyes it would have been so easy to take him up on the offer, but taking the easy option was never going to work if she was going to stand a chance of convincing her mother that a career as a GP wasn't some sort of cop-out. Kevin's mood might not have been dampened, but thoughts of Claudia's mother had certainly had that effect on her mood.

'You think I should stay here because

Kevin Forrester called me brilliant?' She hoped she'd managed to keep her tone light and hadn't come of sounding like her mother, as if the opinion of someone like Kevin didn't hold any weight.

'Not just Kevin. All the patients rave about you, even Mrs Jessop couldn't deny you've helped her. She might not have wanted to listen to your advice, but she took it all the same and that's nothing short of a miracle when it comes to her. Then there's everything you've done for Stacie.' He wrapped his hands around the coffee cup in front of him. 'She left a message for you, by the way.'

'Is she okay?' Claudia was desperate to hear whether Nicola had lived up to her expectations and taken the news of her daughter's engagement as a good thing, despite the circumstances.

'She's fine, she wanted to talk to you really, but you were still with Kevin and I was already out in reception when the call came through, but she said she'd tried your mobile first. Everything seems to have settled down with Greg's dad, so she isn't worried about needing to fly straight out there now.'

'And how did Nicola take the news about her accepting Greg's proposal?'

'She cried with happiness apparently and told Stacie she'd thought Greg was right for her when she'd met him, so she couldn't be more thrilled.' Theo didn't look surprised at Nicola's response. 'She also told Stacie that she's been dreaming about her wedding ever since she was a little girl, and that she'll find a way for her and Danny to be there, whatever it takes. They're not telling Danny yet, and I can tell she still feels guilty, but Nicola seems to have found a way of taking the edge off that too.'

'I'm so pleased. I knew she'd feel so much better with Nicola to support her whilst Greg is away and his father is so ill. I never had any doubt that she'd just want the best for Stacie.' There was that knife twisting in her gut again. As delighted as she was for her friend, she knew if she ever told her mother she was getting engaged, it would barely register on Juliet's radar, except with a look of disdain perhaps, unless she was marrying someone who'd advance her social status. Claudia's mother would certainly never go into raptures at the prospect of being mother of the bride, pigs would sprout wings and fly before that happened.

'Stacie also said she didn't know what she'd have done if you hadn't been here for her over the last few days.' If Theo was trying to weaken her defences, he was doing a pretty good job. 'So you being in St. Finbar's Cross really had made a difference. To us all.'

'I like it here too, but . . . '

'There doesn't have to be a *but*, you know. I love having you around, and not just because I think you're an asset to the surgery.'

'Oh.' It was the second time during their conversation that Claudia had been lost for words.

'I'm going to lay my cards on the

table and tell you that I'd like you to stay. I know that's not in your plan, but at least give it some more thought, please?' Theo paused and she nodded in response, not sure how to confess that although her heart told her to grab the offer with both hands, her head was still fixated on proving something to Juliet. The power her mother had over her was illogical. She didn't even like the woman, yet the desire to make her mother change her view about what Claudia was doing with her life still overrode everything else. She suspected a therapist would have called it a dysfunctional relationship and very unhealthy. Sometimes Claudia was tempted to use much stronger words than that.

'Okay, I promise to think about it.' She forced a smile. Like Kevin before him, she wanted to let Theo down easily. There was no point telling him that as much as she wanted to stay, she wouldn't be able to, just because she had something to prove to a woman it was impossible to please anyway. If she said it out loud it would seem ridiculous and no one who didn't know Juliet would have a chance of understanding.

'Thank you!' Theo looked like she'd handed him a lottery ticket, and she felt another stab — this time of guilt. 'I can't tell you how much that means to me.' Their eyes met again for a second and he leant across the table, kissing her lightly on the lips.

'Theo, I . . . ' She caught her breath as she spoke, after he moved back into his seat.

'I'm sorry, I shouldn't have just kissed you again.' He looked contrite, but then a glimmer of a smile caught at the edge of his lips. 'But I'd be a liar if I didn't admit that I've been tempted to kiss you hundreds of times since the first time I saw you struggling with your cases at the station.'

'Don't remind me!' She laughed; it seemed like light years ago now that she'd refused his offer of a lift in his beaten-up Land Rover. 'It's not that I don't feel the same, either. It's just with not knowing whether I'm going to be here much longer, it makes things a lot more complicated.'

'I understand. But I just want you to know that, even if you don't stay on at the surgery, I'm hoping that you'll be in my life and not just because my sister told me I'd be an idiot if I didn't tell you how I felt!' He smiled again and she longed to return the kiss, but if she gave in to her heart it might just over rule her head and she couldn't let that happen.

'I'm flattered that Janey thinks so highly of me.'

'Like I said, everyone does.' Theo was doing it again, pulling on her heart-strings. Then he went in for the killer blow. 'In fact, that brings me to my next question. Janey wants to know if you'll go to dinner with me at their place on Friday night. The kids have made you something apparently and they're desperate to give it to you.'

'How can I say no to that?' The thought of spending some time with Theo and his lovely family was too much and, for once, her head didn't stand a chance of overruling her heart — even though it might cost her dearly. She'd already accepted that saying goodbye to St. Finbar's Cross wasn't going to be easy when the time came, but she had a horrible feeling that saying goodbye to Theo, and the life and friendships she was beginning to build in this quirky little village, would prove even more difficult.

9

Theo picked Claudia up from the Golden Fleece at seven o'clock on Friday evening. He took her hand in his as she got in to the car.

'You look amazing.' He gave her an appreciative smile, and Claudia was tempted to say *What, this old thing?* — but she smiled instead. She'd never got used to accepting compliments — they'd been few and far between in the past — but she could tell Theo meant what he said. It was a foolish risk, going out with a man she could so easily lose her heart to, when it was just destined to end up broken anyway. It was best not to respond to the compliment; it seemed easier that way.

'I'm really looking forward to seeing Sean and Janey again.' Claudia clicked her seatbelt into place. 'I can't believe the children have made something for me either.'

'Apparently I'm not the only one you've made a big impression on.' Theo looked straight at her, the expression in his dark eyes making her heart do an unexpected flip-flop in response. Not trusting herself to say anything, she just nodded, glad she wasn't the one having to concentrate on the road.

★　★　★

Arriving at Janey and Sean's, the house was lit up like a birthday cake, with lights on all over and music pouring out of an open window upstairs.

'Sorry about the din, Marcus is upstairs tidying his bedroom.' Janey smiled apologetically as she opened the front door. 'He told me he can only work with music playing. Unfortunately, I told him to open the bedroom window to let some air in and the smell of his football socks out! So now the whole neighbourhood can hear his iPod blaring. I blame Sean for getting him a docking station with speakers big enough to hear it three valleys away.' She kissed both of them on the cheek and they went through to the warmth of the house. Late autumn was beginning to cloak the evenings with cold.

'How's Sean?' Theo addressed his sister as she led them through to the kitchen.

'Oh, you know Sean.' Janey's voice sounded tight. 'He's rushing ahead with plans for the adventure centre and not taking enough care of himself. He's been having quite a lot of pain lately, not that he'll admit to it. But I can see it on his face, and I'm the one who hears it when he cries out in pain.'

Theo squeezed her shoulder. 'It's just his way of coping.' He spoke softly as Janey leant against him. 'It's what's got him through since the accident. The man's as stubborn as a mule — and thank goodness for that, or he might have allowed himself to wallow.'

'I know,' Janey sighed, filling up three glasses without even asking them whether they wanted a drink, and leaning on the kitchen counter behind her. 'I just wish he'd be honest enough with himself, and with me, to admit when he's in pain. He snaps at the kids sometimes and I don't think they really understand why. It would be better for everyone if there was just a bit more honesty that life isn't always perfect with a wheelchair in the way.'

'I'll talk to him. See if I can get him to tell me how things really are.' Theo wrapped his arms around Janey, and it was obvious to Claudia just how close the siblings were. She didn't say anything; it wasn't her place to comment on Sean's situation. Despite that, she didn't feel like a spare part or awkward in their company whilst they were talking about something that was so intimate to their family. Yet she would have done with her own family, which said so much about the tenuous relationship she had with her mother.

Suddenly there was a clatter behind them, heralding the arrival of Laura, who'd brought her scooter to a noisy halt on the kitchen tiles.

'What's wrong with Mummy, Uncle Theo?' Laura looked up at the three adults with worried brown eyes.

'I'm just a bit tired, darling,' Janey reassured her daughter, though she was still leaning heavily on Theo for support. 'Why don't you go back through to the playroom, I'll call you for dinner in a little while.'

''Cos I don't want to go and play! Not on my own anyway.' Laura stuck out her bottom lip in the wonderfully petulant way that only little girls could. 'Marcus is playing with his Xbox, and I wanted someone to play Monopoly with.'

'I'll give a game if you like.' Claudia smiled down at the little girl. 'Although I have to tell you that I used to beat my grandmother at Monopoly all the time.'

'Well, you won't beat me, you know!' Laura gave a gap-toothed grin. 'I always win, because I always buy Mayfair and Park Lane, and Marcus is too silly to notice!' Claudia watched the little girl growing more animated as she spoke, and even Janey was managing to smile, despite her obvious worries about Sean.

'Come on then, champ!' Claudia laughed as she followed Laura out of the kitchen. Turning to the others, she added, 'I'll see you later — after I've been thoroughly roasted, by the sound of things!'

Theo smiled in response. His eyes, when they met hers, were so warm that the feeling of being at home in his presence deepened further. She suspected that Theo and Janey could use some time together, without the danger of Laura listening in, to decide exactly how to tackle Sean. So Claudia threw herself on her metaphorical sword, more than happy to suffer the endlessness of a game of Monopoly in order to help her new friends out.

$\star$ $\star$ $\star$

After what seemed like an eternity of sitting cross-legged on the floor, facing a ferociously competitive Laura across the Monopoly board, Claudia finally heard footsteps outside the playroom door.

'Hello, there! If it isn't the beautiful Dr Taylor!' Sean struggled to bend down from his position in the wheel-chair, and managed to plant a clumsy kiss on the top of Claudia's head before returning somewhat unsteadily to an upright position. 'I see my daughter's soundly thrashing you.' He grinned, gesturing towards Claudia's dwindling pile of money, while across the board Laura had lined up rows of hotels.

'Yes, she's a bit of a deadly operator.' Claudia smiled up at Sean, but didn't add that she'd deliberately made some dodgy investments in the hope of finishing the game of Monopoly before midnight.

'Well, Claudia's better at this than you, Dad!' Laura gave her father an accusing look. 'At least she doesn't ask to be the banker and then keep taking money out of the box all the time.' The look on the little girl's face was one of pure indignation. Sean and Claudia exchanged glances and she fought the urge to laugh. Her pint-sized opponent was taking things *very* seriously.

'At least I know where she gets her winning ways from.' Claudia had noticed Laura sneaking an extra five-hundred-pound note out of the bank whenever the need arose, but since it made speedier bankruptcy for Claudia a likely outcome, she'd happily turned a blind eye. After all, cheating at board games was only cheating if you got caught.

'Well, to make up for my previous misdemeanours as the Monopoly banker, I've come to rescue you.' Sean grinned as Claudia let out a sigh of relief that she hadn't meant for anyone to hear. 'Janey says that dinner's ready and so I'm afraid you'll have to abandon the game and come through now.'

'Never mind.' Laura grabbed hold of Claudia's hand as she stood up. 'We can finish the game after dinner.'

'I'm sure Claudia would love that!' Sean gave Claudia a mischievous wink as he spoke.

'Oh I would.' She managed to sound convincing, even to her own ears, although she noticed Sean's raised eyebrows. 'But only if your dad can join in, because I know he was feeling left out.'

'Well, I don't know, I wouldn't want to ruin the hard-fought battle the two of you have been having.' Sean laughed and winked at Claudia again, clearly thinking he'd got out of it.

'He can join in,' Laura said grudgingly. 'But you'll have to help me keep an eye on him because he's a terrible cheat you know!'

'Oh, I think I can manage that. After all, we can't have your dad missing out on all the fun.' It was Claudia's turn to tease Sean, who threw up his hands in defeat, a big smile on his face all the same.

Sean and Claudia were still laughing

when they got to the dining room. It was no good pretending that what she'd found in St. Finbar's Cross — this feeling of coming home — could just be replicated elsewhere. Maybe she should think about staying and stop worrying about her mother's response to the news. After all, Claudia could win the Nobel Prize and Juliet would still find a way of putting her down. The thought that she might allow herself to stay made her feel warm inside. She wouldn't say anything to Theo yet, and she might not be able to commit to staying permanently either yet, but she was more certain with every passing day that she wasn't quite ready to say goodbye. As Claudia took her seat, Theo whispered in her ear.

'Thanks for keeping Laura occupied, I think Janey and I have a plan now. I really don't know what I'd do without you.' Being this close to Theo she could smell the heady scent of his aftershave and feel the warmth of his breath on her neck. The reasons for staying were starting to gather like the layers of moss on the proverbial rolling stone that had suddenly come to a halt. If she allowed herself to stop and settle, that wasn't necessarily a bad thing. Her mother had always made *settling down* sound like dirty words.

'Why's Claudia going so red?' Marcus, who didn't miss a thing, was looking in their direction from his position at the other end of the table.

'Oh, I expect it's the heat of this cannelloni.' Janey smiled as she placed the steaming dish of pasta in the centre of the table.

'Or it's Uncle Theo's electric personality!' Sean was teasing again, the friendship between him and Theo had the depth that Claudia's friendships had never really had. Juliet had never been the sort of mother to arrange sleepovers and, whenever Claudia had brought a friend home, the atmosphere had made them almost as uncomfortable as it had Claudia. Not one of them had asked to come back for a second visit. She'd had friends at university and work colleagues she sometimes went out with later on in life, but there was always a part of herself she kept back. Maybe it was because she didn't want to have to try and live up to anyone's expectations if she got really close to them. Keeping some level of distance meant that no one relied on her, or expected more than she was able to give.

* * *

By the time dinner was over, the table looked unrecognisable from the neatly-laid arrangement they'd sat down to. Sean was clearly in pain at times, and Claudia had seen Theo exchanging looks with his sister when it got too obvious to ignore. The children seemed oblivious, though, which was clearly their father's intention. And the hectic messiness of family life seemed to take the edge off for everyone.

Despite Sean's pain, the four adults

were easy in each other's company, and the laughter flowed as freely as the wine. After dinner, Claudia was spared a return to the Monopoly board, only to be subjected to a team game of charades with boys against girls instead. Sean insisted on choosing his own charades and proceeded to mime *Carry on Doctor* and *Carry on Again Doctor* whilst looking pointedly at Claudia and Theo.

'You're worse than the kids!' Janey said, kissing her husband. Sean winced slightly as he manoeuvred his chair to the side of the room, as if the effort of performing his mime had exhausted him.

'Are you okay?' Theo turned towards him, the colour having drained from his face.

'Just a bit tired I think.' Sean tried to summon up a smile, but it was obvious to Claudia that his face was contorted with pain. 'I think it was the effort of carrying on like a doctor that did it.'

'Why don't you go and get Claudia's present now, kids?' Janey turned towards

Laura and Marcus, who'd been tussling over the next card in the box of charades. Protecting her children seemed to come as second nature to Janey. Claudia had never seen up close what this sort of motherhood looked like — putting them first, come what may.

'Yay!' Laura released the card she'd been fighting her brother for, nearly making him fall backwards in the process. 'Come on Marcus, I need your help to carry it.'

The children disappeared, already racing each other to get upstairs first, so that Janey's cries of *Don't run!* stood little chance of making an impact.

'Have you taken your painkillers?' Theo had moved over to where Sean was sitting.

'They just don't seem to be having as much effect lately.' His brother-in-law spoke quietly, nothing like his normal jokey self. Claudia sighed at the unfairness of it all. Chronic pain could often accompany a spinal cord injury, despite the paralysis it caused. It seemed like a double blow, the body below the injury didn't function in the way it should, but the injury could still cause terrible pain.

'Have you thought any more about moving up to morphine?' Theo turned to look at Janey and Claudia, and then back to Sean. 'I told you before that the meds you're on at the moment are the middle ground for dealing with this sort of thing and that morphine might be a better solution in the long run.'

'I know, but it just has that sound about it.' Sean grimaced again, as he shifted slightly in his chair. 'The sort of drug an addict would sell his left kidney for and I've always just hated that kind of thing. Not only that, but I'm trying to promote a certain sort of lifestyle for others with spinal cord injuries when I set up the centre — to persuade them that they *can* still do the stuff they never thought they would when they got injured. I just don't want to be doing that drugged up to the eyeballs on morphine.'

'So you'd rather sit there in agony?' The impatience in Janey's voice was audible. 'Tell him he's being an idiot, Claudia, he might actually listen to you. Theo and I have tried until we're blue in the face!' She slammed down her glass, red wine slopping over the edge and on to the table.

'I'm not going to call him that and, believe me, I can sympathise with what all of you are saying. In the end everyone just wants what they think is best.' Claudia paused to lean over and squeeze Janey's hand. She knew how hard this was for her new friend, but it was Sean's life and it had to be his decision. 'I can understand why taking morphine worries you too, Sean, but it really can be a good long-term solution and it doesn't need to have the side-effects you are worrying about. I had a patient recently with chronic pain from a broken back she'd suffered years before. She'd been taking tramadol and gradually increasing the dose, but over the years it had just stopped working as well. She'd been told that morphine was the next step up but, like you, she had fears about what that might mean. She thought she wouldn't be able to drive or function as normal, but I reassured her that with the dose I was prescribing she could still do all those things. She came in again last week, to say that since starting the morphine, she'd had her first night of unbroken sleep in more than eight years.' Claudia smiled at Sean, who was still looking unconvinced. 'Look, I'm not saying that drugs are the answer to everything, and maybe you can look at some complementary treatments to run alongside — acupuncture or heat treatment, for example — but just don't write off something that could potentially increase your quality of life hugely because of horror stories you've heard about when morphine's used in the wrong way. It might be the one thing that lets you show everyone at the adventure centre that amazing things are still possible, with the right treatment and the right support.'

'I'll give it a go . . . ' He hesitated as

Janey gasped in response. ' . . . on the condition that Theo looks into a list of complimentary treatments for me, to see what I can be referred for. I want to be able to share that sort of thing with people at the adventure centre, not just compare the number and doses of tablets we're taking.'

'It's a deal.' Theo moved to shake Sean's hand and then turned back to Claudia, kissing her gently on the lips, much to the disgust of Marcus and Laura who'd arrived back in the dining room at the very moment.

'Urgh, Uncle Theo, that is dees-gust-ing!' Marcus pulled a face as Laura voiced what seemed to be their shared opinion for once.

'I'm sorry, guys.' Theo's smile was unshakeable, despite the disapproval of his nephew and niece. 'But Claudia has just performed a small miracle and I wanted to thank her.'

'This is a much nicer way of saying thank-you.' Marcus held up a papier-mâché creation which Claudia couldn't quite identify, whilst Laura pointed towards it with both hands in the style of a conjurer's assistant.

'We made it for you. Do you like it?' Laura looked pointedly in her direction, the weight of expectation written all over her little face.

'I *love* it!' And she did. She might not know what it was, but she loved it all the same. The children had obviously spent a long time making it for her and that touched her heart more than she'd ever thought it would.

'What exactly is it?' Theo, who was already in the children's bad books for the kiss, obviously thought he may as well ask the obvious question. Janey was looking as though she desperately hoped she wouldn't have to try and identify it, and Sean laughed every time he looked towards where his children stood, holding what looked like the remnants of a piñata that had been given the Frankenstein treatment.

'It's a dog, of course!' Marcus, it seemed, was growing increasingly frustrated with his uncle. 'Anyone can see that.'

'Yes, of course, how stupid of me.' Theo didn't quite manage to suppress the smile that accompanied his words. 'Now might I ask why you've made Claudia a dog?'

'In case she gets lonely, silly.' Laura folded her arms across her chest, beginning to lose patience with her uncle too. 'Mummy said she's got no family near here and that she isn't allowed any pets at the hotel either, so we thought this would do until she got somewhere permanent to live. Then she can get a real dog, or a goldfish or something, just so she isn't on her own.'

'Well, I don't know about that, I'm not sure I could ever replace this fine fellow.' Claudia took the surprisingly heavy papier-mâché dog from Marcus. 'Has he got a name?'

'We've been calling him Wilson.' Marcus patted what Claudia assumed was the dog's head, although in all honesty it was quite difficult to tell.

'Wilson.' Claudia put him on the

table and pulled both children into a hug. 'I can't thank you enough for making him for me and I promise I will treasure him for ever.' She meant every word. The arrival of Wilson was one more reason to stay in St. Finbar's Cross and finally free herself from the stranglehold of her mother's opinions. It might have been worthless in monetary terms, but it meant the world to her.

10

In the end, Stacie had ended up taking a few days off work to talk things through properly with her mum and to start making plans to join Greg in Australia. Her return to work the following week was a welcome one and it didn't seem possible that one day soon she might be gone for good. The temporary receptionist they'd had in her absence had done his best, but he'd somehow managed to double book the practice nurse, Helen, with a series of appointments when she was supposed to be running the family planning clinic. It was Stacie herself who Claudia missed the most, though, and she was sure Theo and Helen felt the same. Even the absence of her doorstep-thick sandwiches on the table in the staffroom made the place feel odd. St. Finbar's Cross Surgery just wasn't the same without Stacie at the helm.

'You look fantastic!' Claudia folded Stacie into a hug, as soon as she arrived at the surgery; she really did look transformed from the tearful young woman who Claudia had last seen back at the hotel.

'I'm feeling so much better.' Stacie produced a Tupperware box filled to the brim with sandwiches from her bag. 'I thought you might have been missing these not-so-little beauties!'

'That's brilliant, we've missed your culinary expertise but that's not all we've missed. How's your mum?' Claudia didn't want to intrude too much on what had gone on between Stacie and Nicola. It was enough for her to know that her friend's mum was supporting her, but she was a bit concerned about how someone as selfless as Nicola would take care of herself.

'She's been brilliant, just like you said she would be. The great news is that money doesn't need to be so much of a worry for her either. My stepfather has finally been tracked down and he owes a *lot* of child support, so that's really going to take the pressure off financially.' Stacie frowned slightly for the first time since arriving at the surgery. 'I just wish now that I'd told Mum earlier. I think she was a bit hurt that I didn't tell her before anyone else, but she understands why I told you and she said to tell you that she really wants to cook you a slap-up meal when you're next free; to say thanks.'

'There's no need for that. Although I'd love to see her and Danny again soon, to see if there is anything else I can do to help with the fete. I can't believe how quickly that's coming round either.'

'Neither can I.' Stacie's smile was firmly back where it belonged. 'Danny can't wait. He loves being the centre of attention.'

'It really is brilliant to have you back.' Claudia hugged her friend again, still amazed how close she had become to her colleagues at the medical centre in such a short time.

'Aren't you going to ask me anything else?' Stacie gave her a quizzical look and when Claudia didn't respond with another question, she put her head slightly on one side. 'I felt sure you'd ask about Greg too.'

'I'm so sorry, I was going to ask, but I didn't want to upset you if things with his dad haven't been going so well. It's just so nice to see you you looking so happy again, I didn't want to say anything to bring that down.'

'Well, actually, that's the reason I *am* looking so happy.' Stacie laughed, as if to prove her point. 'You know you said you wished you could wave a magic wand for me to make everything alright? Well, I'm beginning to wonder if you do have mystical powers after all . . .'

'Now, you're just teasing me, standing there with a smile on your face that the Cheshire Cat would be envious of!' Stacie's happiness was infectious, though, and whatever this other news was, Claudia could see how happy it was making her.

'Well, put it this way, if you'd told me all this was going to happen a week ago, I'd never have believed you!' Stacie couldn't stop smiling. 'Greg's dad has been working with a speech and language therapist to see if she could help him get his swallowing back on track and it seems she's nothing short of a miracle worker. She changed the time he eats, so it's whilst his medication is taking maximum effect and he's gained nearly two kilos in the past week as a result.'

'That's fantastic news.' Claudia was smiling now too. It was the best outcome they could have hoped for and exactly what she'd wanted to happen. Medication could only do so much, but with therapeutic support a lot could be achieved by making lifestyle changes and Greg's dad was being given a new lease of life as a result.

'That's not even the best bit!'

'So is this where you tell me you've won a billion dollars on the Australian lottery to set-up your new life together?'

The way things were going, even that seemed suddenly possible to Claudia.

'No, it's much better than that! Greg's mum and dad had apparently been talking for a while about coming back to the UK, to be nearer his mum's sisters, so she'd have some support with looking after Bill, Greg's dad. And now that things seem to be back on an even keel again, with his health, they want to make it happen and soon. So it looks like you're going to be stuck with me around here, after all!'

'They're moving here?' Claudia could barely take it in, but she could vouch to Greg's parents that there was nowhere better they could settle than St. Finbar's Cross.

'Greg's flying back at the end of the week to find a house for them all to rent in Bassington and we'll look for somewhere to move into together after the wedding, either in St. Finbar's Cross, or somewhere nearby. Either way, both of us will be less than twenty minutes from our families and that to me is much better than any lottery win!'

'I couldn't agree more. So is Greg going to get a job locally too?'

'The hotel chain he works for want to keep him on, so they've offered him the General Manager's post of the hotel he's just finished renovating.' Stacie laughed again. 'It's like I said, it really is as though someone has come along and waved a wand to make all the wishes I had come true. Well almost all of them.'

'There's still something else you want? That seems like more than enough miracles to me for one week.'

'I know, I'm being greedy, but this one is as much about you as it is about me. You're a brilliant doctor and an even better friend. You know that, don't you?' Stacie finally moved towards her desk, the official start of the day would wait for no-one and there'd be patients knocking on the door if they didn't open up in time. 'So that's my last wish, that you realise that life in St. Finbar's Cross could be perfect for you too and that a certain Dr Theo Harrison could be a big part of that, if only you'd let him in.'

'I won't say I'm not flattered that you're prepared to use up a wish hoping that I'll stay around.' Claudia chose to ignore the comment about Theo, in case what she said gave too much away about how she was feeling. She was determined to count the blessings they'd already had, and a weight had been lifted from her shoulders seeing Stacie looking so much more like her old self. 'Talking of Theo, he told me to give you a big kiss from him, but I'll let that wait until he's here. He's had to go to a meeting in Bassington, so he won't be in until about eleven, but Helen will be in just before ten for the weight loss clinic this morning. So it's just you and me for now.'

'Against the world?' Stacie smiled and Claudia shook her head.

'Not any more, you've got plenty of people on your side and soon you'll be

surrounded by a whole new family too.'
St. Finbar's Cross certainly seemed to
be living up to its reputation of making
wishes come true, and Claudia felt the
familiar pull the place was having on
her all over again.

★   ★   ★

Claudia scanned the list of patients for
the morning and let go of a long sigh
when she realised Mrs Jessop was
among them, her good mood evaporat-
ing a bit more swiftly than she'd hoped
it would. Not that she couldn't handle
awkward patients and even cantankerous ones, but there was something
about Mrs Jessop that reminded Claudia of her mother. They were nothing
alike physically, of course. Juliet would
be mortified to be seen with a hair out
of place and she'd always been weight-
conscious to the point of obsession. It
was more to do with the way she could
never see the good in any situation, a
habit Mrs Jessop evidently shared. She

was probably coming in to tell Claudia again that she'd been wrong about the Baker's cyst or to regale her with what a disaster the befriending service had been. Either way, it wasn't an appointment that she was looking forward to and even a morning taken up with routine consultations for rashes, bunions and lower back pain seemed preferable to that. The hands of the clock slithered closer to Mrs Jessop's eleven twenty appointment and Claudia thanked goodness she was running more or less to time. Keeping Mrs Jessop waiting beyond her allotted time would just add fuel to the fire.

'Morning, Mrs Jessop, what can I do for you?' Claudia forced herself to smile as the older woman came into the consulting room and, if she hadn't know better, she'd have sworn Mrs Jessop was smiling too.

'I've just come in to see if I can get a prescription for something to help me get things moving. I'm taking co-codamol for the arthritis in my shoulder and it works for the pain, but it has *other effects*.' She mouthed the last two words almost silently, obviously uncomfortable talking about that sort of thing in too much detail, even to her doctor.

'Absolutely. It's a fairly common side-effect of codeine and I can prescribe you something mild like fybogel or senna, or we can give you a syrup that can be a bit more effective with these types of painkiller?'

'I think I better go for the syrup.' Mrs Jessop seemed much more amenable than Claudia remembered and she wondered if something significant had happened to brighten her patient's mood, or whether she just wanted the consultation to be over as quickly as possible.

'Have you thought any more about a shoulder replacement?' Claudia looked back at Mrs Jessop's notes on the computer. 'I see your previous doctor discussed this with you?'

'Yes. And Dr Harrison has been on at me to think about it too. But my husband went downhill after an operation and he died within six months, he was only in his late fifties. I just don't want to have to go through that if I don't have to.' There was none of the aggression in Mrs Jessop's tone that there had been at her last visit. Something had definitely changed.

'You know that Mr Jessop's heart failure wasn't related to the operation though, don't you?' Claudia was really risking it now, challenging Mrs Jessop's long-held views.

'So they say, but I just don't like hospitals after all of that.' Mrs Jessop sighed. 'I thought with having a husband a good few years younger than me, that I wouldn't be the one left alone. It was a big shock.'

'I can imagine.' Claudia spoke softly, anxious not to stop Mrs Jessop now that she had finally opened up. Theo had told her he suspected that loneliness was at the root of some of Mrs Jessop's behaviour, but it was obvious now that he'd been right. 'What about the Baker's cyst. Has that all calmed down a bit now?'

'Yes, you were right about that. I'm sorry if I seemed a bit short with you last time I was here, it's just that lumps and things can be really worrying when you're on your own with no-one to talk to about it and to reassure you that it really will all be okay. I just didn't want to think you were dismissing it out of hand without checking it out properly first.' Mrs Jessop shook her head. 'I know that's not what you did and that you know exactly what questions to ask to see if it is likely to be anything sinister, but I knew I'd still convince myself when I got home that it could be a tumour or something. I just need someone around to talk sense into me sometimes!' Mrs Jessop was *definitely* smiling this time.

'And what about the befriending service? How did it go when they sent someone round?' Claudia steeled herself for the old Mrs Jessop to return and give her both barrels about what a disaster that had been.

'Well, that's the other reason I'm here actually. To say thank you.' Claudia was sure she saw a flush of colour highlight Mrs Jessop's cheeks as she spoke.

'It went well then?'

'They sent round a Mr Hayward, Roger.' There was no denying it now, Mrs Jessop's cheeks were unmistakably flushed with pink. 'I thought it would be some teenager trying to get credit for their university application or a bored housewife wanting something to occupy her now her kids have grown up.'

'I take it you were wrong?' Claudia was almost tempted to pinch herself to check that she wasn't dreaming all of this. It seemed far too good to be true.

'Completely. Roger's only a few years younger than me as it happens. Like my late husband.' The blush deepened as she made the comparison. 'He was only supposed to come round once a week, but we got on so well and he loves gardening too. He moved into a flat when he was widowed, so he doesn't have his own garden anymore and he just loves helping me out with mine.'

'That's marvellous.' Claudia wasn't going to push her luck and ask if romance was on the cards, but a big part of her hoped that it was. It was nice to think that two people who'd clearly been lonely could find something like that again. A sort of fairy tale ending to what seemed to have been quite a sad story for them both in recent years. Whatever Mr Hayward had brought into Mrs Jessop's life, Claudia would have loved to be able to bottle it. If it could turn someone like Mrs Jessop around so dramatically, it had the potential to cure an awful lot of ills. Depression could be more debilitating than physical illness and Mrs Jessop had clearly been very low since her husband's death. But with a new friend, someone to share her passion for gardening with, and to use as a sounding board for some of her worries, she was like a new woman.

'I feel like I've got things to look

forward to now. He's taking me to the pictures on Tuesday to see the new Maggie Smith film. It's been years since I've been and I'd forgotten how much of a difference it can make to just get out and do things sometimes.' Mrs Jessop actually reached out and put her hand over Claudia's. 'I just wish I'd listened and done it a long time ago. Still, things are meant to be sometimes and I might not have been paired with Roger if I'd phoned at some other time.'

'I probably shouldn't say this as a doctor, since I'm supposed to take a scientific view of everything, but I think some things are definitely meant to be. So maybe it *was* fate that you called at the same time Roger started to volunteer.'

'Fate and a little push from a well-meaning GP.' Mrs Jessop reached down into her handbag and pulled out a bag of what looked to Claudia like muddy onions. 'These are for you.'

'Oh. Thanks.'

'Don't look like that, Doctor, they're autumn planting bulbs. You need to plant them as soon as possible and they'll come up in the spring.'

'That's so thoughtful of you.' Claudia smiled and wondered if she could plant them around the trees in the surgery car park, since she had no garden of her own. Would she be around in spring to see them come up? There was no denying now that she wanted to be. Mrs Jessop bringing in the bulbs was just one more reason to stay in the village, one more piece of the jigsaw that had come together to let her know that staying in St. Finbar's Cross was the right thing to do, whatever her mother thought.

'It's nothing compared with what you've done for me, Doctor.' Mrs Jessop stood up, taking the prescription that Claudia had printed off for her. 'Just make sure you don't let me down and forget to plant them. You youngsters seem to think that attractive gardens happen all by themselves, but they don't you know, it takes a lot of hard work.'

'I'm sure it does and your garden is testament to that. I promise to get them planted, thanks again Mrs Jessop.' Claudia smiled to herself as her patient closed the door behind her. Glad as she was to see Mrs Jessop so much happier, it was a relief to know that some of the old feistiness was still there, even if it was only when it came to ensuring that those bulbs would get planted in time.

11

The autumn fete in St. Finbar's Cross always had a charitable theme. Theo told Claudia that the committee liked to focus on causes close to the community's heart. In previous years, the fundraising had helped to pay for new playground equipment at the primary school, to replace the antiquated sound system in the church hall and even to buy a travel agency gift voucher so that Sean and Janey's first family holiday after the accident would be paid for by the autumn fundraiser. If Claudia had needed any more convincing that this was the sort of community that would do anything to help one of its members, then the autumn fundraiser would have been in it. As it was, she was still recovering from Mrs Jessop's transformation, when the day of the fete rolled round. As promised, she'd spent a whole Saturday morning the previous week putting in the bulbs that Mrs Jessop had given her, which promised to decorate the surgery car park in a riot of colour come the spring.

It was early on the following Saturday when Stacie came to meet Claudia at the Golden Fleece Hotel, so they could head off and start setting things up at the fete. The church hall had been booked to house the event, should the weather be too cold or rainy. As it was she'd woken up to a glorious autumn day, with bright blue skies and not a cloud to be spotted. The committee had texted all the stall holders to say they should set up outside, but the advice was to wrap up warm and bring a hot flask of tea. After all, despite the unseasonably good weather, it was still November.

'How's everything going with the big house hunt and the wedding plans?' Claudia spoke to Stacie as they climbed into the front of her car, the back seat rammed full of raffle and tombola prizes. 'I've hardly had time to catch you at the surgery lately, what with Theo disappearing for meetings all the time. I seem to have had back to back patients.'

'I know and I'm sorry that I didn't get a chance to come and help you with the planting last weekend.' Stacie gave her a rueful smile. 'Only since Greg's arrived back in the UK, we seem to have been spending our time alternating between looking at houses for his parents to rent and looking at wedding venues. At least he's got accommodation at the hotel, until we get our own place after the wedding. And that seems to have solved the wedding venue dilemma too, we get such good rates to hold the wedding at Greg's hotel that we'd be silly not too. Being a new hotel there's no waiting list yet either, so we're going to go for a Christmas wedding to give his parents a few weeks to settle in. There are a still a few things to sort out, as we haven't quite found the right house for them yet, but all in all it's going pretty well.'

'That's great, and don't give the planting a minute's thought, all of that is far more important. Like I told you all those weeks ago, if it's meant to be, you'll find a way. And you have!' Claudia almost laughed to herself. Since when had she been qualified to give out relationship advice? She and Theo had something, but she still wasn't entirely sure what it was, especially as he'd done a disappearing act several times over the past week, citing *urgent meetings*. He was usually so open and it had been strange for him not to give any indication of what was going on. The suspicious side of Claudia couldn't help thinking there must be more to his absences from the surgery than he was saying. Still, that was a worry for another day. Right now she'd promised to run the tombola stall with Stacie, and rumour had it that the autumn fete was so busy it was highly unlikely to give her a moment's thinking time anyway.

*   *   *

Just as expected the fete was packed with people, from the moment the gate opened. There were lots of stalls in the acre of paddock to the side of the church, which had been freshly mown for the occasion, despite the lateness of the season, and which looked a bit on the churned-up side as a result. The stalls were selling everything from sweets and bric-a-brac to high-end copper sculptures by a local artist, and all of the stallholders had paid a fee to be there, as well as a percentage of their profits, towards the event's fundraising target. Some of the stalls — like the one Stacie and Claudia were running — would be donating all of their takings, but the variety of products on offer made for a big draw and visitors from well beyond the village itself were streaming through the gates in droves.

Nicola and Danny were running a 'splat the rat' stall, where a soft toy rat was posted into the top of a piece of plastic piping and the aim was to hit it with a rubber mallet as it emerged from the other end. Winners and losers alike were then able to claim a prize from the four lucky dip buckets, according to how many rats they'd managed to splat. There was lots of shouting and laughter, and, from where Claudia was standing, it appeared very difficult to hit the target. It didn't seem to stop people from having fun though and the queue to have a go was the longest at the fete. Danny's smiling face and shouts of 'Go on, splat that rat!' were probably a big part of the draw too. Helen, the practice nurse, was doing face painting, half the Smithson family from the Golden Fleece Hotel were running the mulled cider stall and there was a cake table, just to the left of that, laden with all sorts of delights, including scones almost bursting open with Devonshire double cream and deep red strawberry jam. Claudia had promised herself one if there were any left by the time she'd finished helping

Stacie. They might not have been the healthiest of snacks but, as she always told her patients, everyone deserved a treat now and then.

* ★ ★

Claudia had worried that it might be cold, but in her ski-jacket and with a steady flow of customers to the stall, she was actually feeling quite warm. Theo turned up just in time to start the auction of promises. He looked harassed, at first, as if he'd run all the way from wherever it was he'd had his latest meeting, but he soon settled into his stride. Whether it was the way the mulled cider was flowing on the Smithson's stall or not, Claudia couldn't be sure, but, whatever it was, the bids were soon flying in for the promises on offer. Claudia had paid in advance for her riding lesson on Mable, because of the issues with insurance, but Theo had finally come up with another idea that he could contribute to the auction itself. Deciding to pair up with Claudia, and her offer to cook a meal for a dinner party of up to eight people, he'd offered his services as a sort of combined waiter and butler. When he'd read out the promise, there'd been a flurry of conversation amongst the people standing in front of the platform where he was taking the bids. There were several people bidding at first but, as the price began to rise, two blonde women started to go head-to-head, eventually raising the price for Theo and Claudia's combined services to over five hundred pounds. Although she suspected that the final figure had very little to do with her offer to cook the food.

'We should have auctioned Theo off, we'd have had enough to replace the whole church roof.' She turned to Stacie, who was eating her second hot dog of the day, making up for lost time since the morning sickness had abated.

'Ah, well, bid as they might, they're on to a loser. He only has eyes for you.' Stacie laughed at the expression which must have crossed Claudia's face. 'Oh come on, don't tell me you think none of us have realised how close you two have got? He never stops talking about you for a start. And then there's Janey and Sean, of course, telling anyone who will listen that you make the perfect couple.' Stacie gesticulated towards where Sean was positioned in his wheelchair, to the side of where the auction was taking place, with Janey right behind him. Laura and Marcus had seized the opportunity to play 'splat the rat', whilst the auction took place, oblivious of whether their shouts of '*Got him!*' and '*Missed!*' might drown out their Uncle Theo.

'Oh, I'm not sure about that. I'm sure Theo just sees me as a work colleague, or maybe a friend.' Claudia was glad of the opportunity to turn slightly away from Stacie and watch as the next lot in the auction, afternoon tea for two at Bassington's swankiest hotel, opened for bidding.

'Yep, sure, and there go a herd of flying pigs!' Stacie ignored the next auction item and pointed towards the sky to the right of them, before suddenly dropping her hand back down to her side. 'Oh gosh, it's Greg, he's just coming through the gates over there. That's him, the tall guy with the dark hair. He did say he might try and come down if he could, but I wasn't expecting him to really. I haven't got ketchup on my chin, have I?' Stacie wiped some non-existent sauce off her face as she spoke.

'No, you look wonderful. I can manage the stall now. Everyone seems far too engrossed in the auction at the moment to bother with us anyway. I can always rope in Theo to give me a hand after he's finished if it gets busy again. I don't think it's a good idea for you to be on your feet all day in any case. Go on, go and see him.'

Stacie didn't need any further encouragement and Claudia watched as she almost ran towards the infamous Greg. In turn, he looked equally delighted to see her, twirling her round in a little circle before setting her gently back on the ground as though she were made of china. Stacie had said they still had some details to work through before the wedding plans and his parents move could be finalised, but it was obvious they were meant to be together.

* * *

'I bet you didn't expect to see us here?' Claudia had been so fixated on watching Greg and Stacie, that she hadn't notice anyone approach the stall. Even before she looked up into the face of the person whose voice she recognised so well, she knew exactly who it was.

'Mum.' If there'd been a seat behind the stall, she'd have collapsed on to it. Instead she put one hand out to steady herself. The last time they'd seen each other, they'd had a furious row. Tempted as she was to keep up the silent treatment that had prevailed since then, she remembered the promise she'd made to her father and forced herself to hold her mother's gaze.

'Darling, I've told you a million times that I hate the word '*mum*', you're a grown-up now so there's no reason not to simply call me Juliet. But if you must insist on referring to me with a label, I much prefer Mother to Mum, as well you know.'

'Sorry, you just took me completely by surprise.' Thirty seconds in and Claudia was already apologising for being herself, when she'd sworn after their last row that this time she wouldn't back down until her mum was the one to say sorry. If she'd thought living in St. Finbar's Cross might have strengthened her resolve on that front, then she'd been sadly mistaken.

'You can call me Dad, or whatever you like, it's just lovely to see you.' Her father had manoeuvred himself behind the stall and was giving her a slightly awkward hug, probably because he could sense the distaste radiating off his wife as much as Claudia could. It was only for his sake that she was being cordial to her mother at all.

'I do wish you wouldn't do that in public.' Juliet looked as though he'd painted himself blue and danced an Irish jig, rather than just giving the daughter he hadn't seen for months a quick hug. The fact that she was a psychiatrist never ceased to amaze Claudia. How the woman could be trusted with helping other people to sort out their own thoughts and tangles of emotion, when her own ideas were such a twisted version of normality, Claudia would never know.

'What on earth are you doing in St. Finbar's Cross?' Claudia slipped her hand back down by her side, surreptitiously crossing her fingers and offering up a silent prayer that Theo wouldn't choose that moment to end the auction and wander over, or worse still shout across to ask if the couple standing over by the tombola were going to join in and make a bid. She could just imagine her mother's reaction to that.

'Well, that's funny, because we're here

to ask you exactly the same. Just what is it that *you* are doing here?' Juliet cast her eyes around as she said the word 'here', as though she were grasping for some reason, any reason, why her daughter might be standing behind a tombola stall, in a Devonshire village, on a Saturday afternoon in November.

'Working as a locum most of the time, which you know.' Claudia just about held back the urge to sigh in response to the look that crossed her mother's face. 'But, right now, I'm helping with a fundraiser to support my friend's little brother, who has cystic fibrosis, so they can plan some fun days out and for him to have a holiday with his family.'

'Your *friend*?' Juliet made it sound as if Claudia had referred to some kind of alien life form. 'We were concerned that you'd spent a bit too long in this odd little place and now that I hear mention of the word *friends*, I know we were definitely right to step in.'

'So you've driven down from Manchester to stage an intervention?' Claudia shook her head. She might not like her mother but she had to admire the woman's tenacity. She was so determined for Claudia to be 'more than just a GP' as she'd so often put it, that she'd come all this way to persuade her — or most likely to *tell* her — that it was time to move on. Maybe Juliet had wiped the memory of their last row about Claudia's career, and her right to live her own life, from her mind. Even if she hadn't, she certainly hadn't learnt anything from the experience about the way to handle things with her daughter. They were never going to agree, and in a weird sort of way it was a relief. It meant Claudia could stop trying if she wanted to.

'Not quite all the way from Manchester just for that.' Her father gave her an apologetic look, an unspoken understanding on his face. 'Your mother booked us both into a conference at the Royal College of Physicians in London next week, but we thought we'd pop in and see you beforehand, since you're only around four hours from there. But they told us at your hotel that this is where we'd find you.'

'It wasn't a case of popping in from that distance, she's not an idiot, Geoffrey.' Juliet looked at her husband in a way that suggested *he* was the only idiot anywhere nearby. 'You promised me you wouldn't just end up stuck forever in the first backwater you came to, Claudia. But here you are helping out on a stall at some out-of-season village fair, like someone with nothing better to do with their time, looking far too comfortable about the whole thing.'

'Is it really a crime to be comfortable?' Claudia looked from her mother to her father and back again. She noticed an almost in perceivable shake of her father's head but, despite that, he didn't have enough courage to voice the opinion out loud. Maybe it was time for Claudia to speak out, to leave her mother in no doubt this time that, however much she interfered, she wouldn't be able to change the way her daughter thought about things.

'It's a crime to settle for less than you can achieve.' Juliet was warming to her theme and shaking her finger in the way she always had when Claudia refused to see sense, as she saw it. Anyone who didn't agree with Juliet was swept aside by her mother's single-mindedness, and Claudia's father just seemed to stop having a point of view altogether over the years.

'What if I like it here? Isn't that enough? It doesn't always have to be about achieving more than the next person, you know, or having the sort of career other people will remember.' Claudia had a sudden desire to stamp her foot. Her mother's uncanny knack of making her feel like the child no-one listened to, always brought out the worst in her.

'You've got opportunities other people would die for. Just say the word and I can line you up an interview with any hospital you like.' Juliet brushed an imaginary crumb off the silk scarf she was wearing. 'Even your plan to go and practise *general* medicine somewhere a bit more challenging would be better than this. Either way you have to get out, before the demands of people who've probably never left the county, never mind the country, tie you to a place like this.'

'It's not just the place, it's the people.' Claudia wasn't sure why she was arguing, she was a grown-up who could make her own decisions. Her mother would never change her mind if she lived to be a hundred and twenty, anyway, but Claudia couldn't seem to help herself; she so wanted both her parents to understand why St. Finbar's Cross was special.

'Oh for goodness sake, don't tell me you've met someone and you're staying here because you think you're *in love*?' The habit her mother had of taking perfectly ordinary words and making them sound like something else entirely was one that Claudia had happily pushed to the back of her mind since she'd last seen her. Only now it was coming back to her in an unwelcome rush.

'It's got nothing to do with that.' She hoped her face wouldn't betray her, silently praying even harder that Theo wouldn't come over and give the game away. They hadn't talked about anything as deep as being in love but, if their chemistry was as obvious as Stacie had made out, it would just add fuel to Juliet's already raging fire.

'Leave the girl alone, Juliet. It's none of our business if she's courting or not.' Her father smiled in a way that made her want to really upset her mother by hugging him again, so hard that the buttoned-up Juliet might never get over such a public display of affection. They'd both come to parenthood at a relatively late age and her father had such a wonderfully old-fashioned turn of phrase sometimes, as if he'd just stepped out of a period drama. The unfortunate part was that her mother treated him as if he were someone who lived below stairs and had mistakenly found himself in the upper echelons where she resided. What a way to live your life, married to a woman who'd looked down her nose at you for the past forty-odd years and spent her life trying to turn you into something you didn't want to be. Claudia felt another rush of affection towards her father, tempered with a big dollop of sympathy.

'Of course it's our business if she's seeing someone. We invested a fortune in her education, not to mention the other sacrifices I made. I didn't do all of that so she could become a GP in the middle of nowhere and marry some country bumpkin with even less ambition than she's got.'

'For heaven's sake, *Mother*.' Claudia placed heavy emphasis on the word this time around, although there were plenty of other names she was tempted to call her. 'I haven't seen you for months, since the last time we ended up shouting the odds at each other, and I certainly didn't ask you to turn up here and start telling me how to live my life. Although why I should expect you to change the habit of a lifetime I'll never know.'

'Geoffrey, are you going to let her speak to me like that?' Juliet looked pointedly at her husband, who gave a half-hearted shrug.

'I've always thought it best not to get in between two women having a heated discussion.'

'We're having an argument, Dad. And I wish for once people in this family would call things what they are and stop pretending that we're some sort of functional family. Put it this way, if I was one of Mum's clients, I'd be asking for my money back.' Claudia watched her mother's face change as she said the words, her mouth opening and closing like a fish out of water, before she managed to respond.

'How dare you bring my profession into disrepute?' Her mother's shrill voice was carrying across the paddock now and a few people towards the back of the crowd, who'd been watching the auction, turned round to look at them.

'We're leaving right now, Geoffrey, I don't need to hear another word of this.'

'But I thought we were going to speak to Claudia about, you know, the in . . . ' Her father was cut off in mid-flow.

'Only if we were confident that she might use it for something worthwhile, so she could go and work in Alaska or somewhere, like she promised!' Her mother shook her head with considerable vigour. 'But as it seems she's decided to stay in this dead-end town, there's nothing more that needs to be said.'

'But . . . ' Her father was doing his best to protest, more so than she'd seen him try for a long time, but he was on to a losing battle.

'No buts! Come on, Claudia has made it clear that we're not welcome here.' Her mother was already striding back towards the gate and her father gave her hand a quick squeeze before letting it go again.

'Sorry darling, you know what she gets like when she's in one of these moods.'

'I do, Dad.' Claudia sighed as her father made to go after his wife. 'The trouble is, she's always in one of those moods.'

12

'I'm sorry I didn't get a chance to talk to you after the fete yesterday.' Theo brought in two very fancy-looking coffees to the conservatory that over-looked the field at the back of his house. Claudia had been sitting in the little sun trap the glass walls provided, whilst he made the coffees, watching Mable moving around to eat the best patches of grass. How simple life must be when you had no-one's expectations to live up to.

'No, it was my fault. I had to rush off when Stacie and Greg offered to look after the stall.' Claudia felt the warmth seep into her hands as she picked up the coffee cup.

'Yes, she said you looked terrible and that you had a splitting headache. I was going to come down to the hotel to check on you, but Stacie said you just wanted to be on your own?'

'I did have a headache, but it was more of an excuse to get away from everyone before I fell apart in front of them. You know, just one of those really bad days you want to forget?' Her eyes met his briefly and she could tell he wasn't his usual self either. Maybe Sean was in pain again. He'd looked okay at the fete but, as she'd found out that evening at his and Janey's house, Sean was pretty adept at hiding things.

'Yes, I know exactly what you mean, I've had one of two of those days myself lately.'

'Is it Sean?'

'No, thanks goodness. The morphine seems to be doing the trick on that front and Janey still thinks you're the best thing to happen to St. Finbar's Cross in a very long time.' Theo sighed. 'But other than that I think it's been about the worst week I can remember for a while. I think I'm definitely in the running for being the village's biggest loser.'

'No way!' Claudia laughed despite herself. Theo was a hero in the village, it was obvious from the way people spoke about him, and the last thing anyone would accuse him of was being a loser. 'If we're talking about losers, I can beat you hands-down in those stakes, any day. My Saturday afternoon ended up with my mother belittling me for the millionth time and her storming off in a huff, with my dad in hot pursuit, after she'd told me I was wasting my life.'

'Hmm.' Theo puffed out his cheeks. 'Under normal circumstances I'd hand you the prize for having had the worst week, but not this time.'

'I still can't believe you've had a less successful week than me.'

'Try me.'

'Come on then, Dr Harrison, tell me exactly what's so bad that you think you can beat the horror of one of my mother's lectures. I know you've never met her, but lots of people who have would rather wrestle with an anaconda than meet up with her again.'

'She does sound difficult, but I still think I'd rather take her on than repeat my week. There's only so many times I can try to persuade my ex-wife to give me a bit more time to find the money to buy her out of the surgery.' Theo looked suddenly defeated. 'Did I say *ask* her? I meant beg.'

'Oh gosh, I didn't realise she still owned a share. Is that something she's asked for out of the blue?'

'I bought her out of the house when we split up, but she said she wanted to leave her share of the surgery buildings as they were. She said it was an investment for the future, part of her pension fund.' Theo took a sip of his coffee, tiredness etched on his face. 'Only now she's met someone else and she wants to move to Paris with him. So she wants the money yesterday. She was always like that, making decisions without letting me know and then just expecting me to jump to attention and come up with the goods when she decided to let me in on the plan.'

'She can't just do that, though, can she?'

'Unfortunately she owns seventy percent of the building, because she put some extra money into it when her father died. She's already found a buyer if I can't cover what they're offering. The new owner would want me to rent their seventy percent back off them, but the figures they're quoting just don't stack up, we couldn't afford to keep the surgery running like that. So I haven't really got a lot of choice.'

'Can you borrow some money to buy her out?'

'I've approached the bank, but I had to take on quite a big debt to buy her out of the house and they're not willing to support such a big risk for a small surgery. I even spoke to the Trust, but if I can't do anything to stop Sara's plans, it seems everyone thinks the best thing we could do is to join up with Bassington surgery and for our patients to be transferred over there.'

'Oh no. Don't they realise how many of the patients in the village depend on the surgery? I know Bassington is only a couple of miles away, but it's going to make life really difficult for some our more elderly and disabled patients.'

'It means so much to me to hear you use the world '*our*'. You're the first person I've spoken to this week who understands why it means so much to me and who doesn't seem to see everything in terms of pound signs. I know Helen and Stacie will feel the same way, but I've put off mentioning anything so far. I've been going to meetings all over the place to try and sort things out, but I'm going to have to come clean sooner or later.'

'Stacie's going to be upset too. She was just saying at the fete how glad she is that she's got a stable job, so that she and Greg can pay for the wedding themselves and set up home afterwards, without putting any more pressure on either set of parents. Greg's got a good job sorted out over here, but with him moving half way around the world to be with her and the prospect of not living at home with Nicola and Danny anymore, I think she just really wants some things to stay the same.' Claudia twisted the silver bracelet on her wrist. If only she was in a position to help Theo out, but, despite her mother's claims about the fortune they'd spent on her education, Claudia had paid most of her way through university and her student debt wouldn't be entirely cleared for a while yet. There was the cottage in Ramsbottom, on the outskirts of Manchester, that she'd rented out when she moved down to Devon, but she couldn't see a bank being willing to lend her enough to buy into the surgery either. It was something she could look into, but it wouldn't be helpful to mention it to Theo now, only to pile more disappointment on top if it came to nothing. Still it made it all crystal clear in her own head; the thought of leaving St. Finbar's Cross, even to go just a couple of miles up the road to Bassington, was horrifying. She wanted to stay, and not just for the short term.

'I know she'll be worried, that's why I haven't mentioned it to the others yet. I keep thinking about Stacie and picturing the look on her face when I tell her.' Theo grimaced. 'It's been keeping me up at night since I found out. The only thing that cheered me up at the fete was seeing how attentive Greg was. I'm just hoping that he'll step up to the mark and she won't have to worry about finding a new job until after the wedding. If she has to work a long way away from here and settle into a new role, as well as planning everything and helping Greg's parents get settled into their new place, it'll cut down on the time she has to spend with Danny and Nicola even more.'

'I'm sure Greg will help her shoulder the burden.' Claudia forced a smile, hoping it would turn out to be as simple as that, but the last thing Theo needed was any more doom and gloom.

They had to find a way to keep the surgery open.

'And what about you? Will you leave us now that you know the surgery probably won't be here in a few months' time?' Theo looked desperate and, even if she hadn't already reached her decision, she'd have been tempted to tell him that she'd stay and help him fight for the surgery. As it was, her answer was easy.

'I'm not going anywhere. If you still want me to stay that is?'

'I've never wanted anything more.' Despite his worries, Theo was smiling. And, as he pulled her into his arms, everything in Claudia's world suddenly felt a little bit better too.

Theo was true to his word. Come Monday morning, he made the announcement at the end of the regular staff meeting that the surgery was under threat of closure, unless he could find a way of buying Sara out, or find another suitable premises almost immediately — the latter option seeming even less likely than the first. Claudia had spent Sunday evening, after she'd gone back to the hotel, trying to find out if there were any banks that would loan her the four hundred thousand pounds she needed to buy Theo's ex-wife out of the surgery. The most she'd been able to find was a bank who might be willing to lend her two hundred and fifty thousand towards it, but only if she put her cottage in Ramsbottom up for collateral. Maybe, if Theo could raise the other hundred and fifty thousand, between them they could pull it off.

Stacie's reaction had surprised them all, not because she wasn't passionate about trying to save the surgery, but because of what she was willing to do in order to make that happen.

'I phoned Mum as soon as I came out of the meeting and we're agreed.' Stacie looked at Theo and Claudia in turn, her arms crossed against her chest as though she meant business.

'About what?' Theo, who still gave the appearance that sleep was largely eluding him, laid a hand on her arm. It was the measure of the man, as far as Claudia was concerned, that he seemed much more worried about his staff and patients than he did his own livelihood.

'We don't need the money the fete raised that badly. Like I told Claudia before, the CSA have finally caught up with my stepfather and managed to squeeze some child maintenance out of him, so Mum should be better off soon than she has been in a long while, even without me living at home. Danny would rather have the surgery close by and keep the same doctors than go swimming with dolphins. We're all agreed, we want you to have the money towards the Save the Surgery Fund.'

'I don't think . . . ' Theo barely got the first couple of words out before his receptionist cut him off again.

'It's the best way to do it. This community have always been good at fundraising.' Stacie's arms were still firmly folded. 'I'm going to set up a Facebook page and Twitter account as soon as I get home. We can't take this lying down and I'm sure Greg will help too, he's a whizz at all that sort of stuff.'

'That's amazingly generous of you.' This time Theo appeared equally determined not to be cut off. His body language mirrored Stacie's and it looked a bit like a Mexican standoff to Claudia, neither one wanting to back down. 'But let's face it, it's a huge amount of money we need to raise and there's no way in the world that I'm going to allow you to take anything out of the money collected for Danny. Everyone at the fete was donating with him in mind, for a start, and I couldn't live with myself if I thought we'd deprived him of the chance to have some fun.'

'Theo's right, it wouldn't be fair for Danny to make that sort of sacrifice, even if he wants to.' Claudia put an arm around Stacie's shoulders. 'But I think raising the plight of the surgery on social media won't do any harm. Perhaps some generous billionaire will read it and step in to donate the funds we need. Or maybe if we can apply enough pressure, the Trust might even change their minds and do something to help us out.' Claudia wished she could believe that last part, but she wasn't going to be the one to take away Stacie's hope. She needed to feel like she was doing something to try and stop the surgery closing — they all did.

'We've just heard the news, it's all over the village!' Mrs Jessop burst through the doors of the surgery, like a bull at the gate, trailing a couple of other ladies behind her.

'Nothing's definite, but I must admit I wasn't expecting the news to be made public yet or to travel quite so fast.' Theo shot Stacie a look. Nicola obviously wasn't the only one she'd told. It was inevitable that word would spread quickly in such a tight knit community anyway.

'We can't lose this place. So many of us rely on having a doctor in the village and the other services you provide.'

One of the other women shook her head as she spoke. 'We've got to do something to stop it.'

'Too right we have!' Mrs Jessop was not someone to be argued with at the best of times. 'We need a council of war and we thought this might come in handy whilst we have the first strategy meeting. My infamous coffee and walnut cake.' She removed a large cake box from her shopping bag.

'I'm sure it's delicious and I'm not saying that we shouldn't have a meeting to see if there are any ideas we can come up with to save the surgery.' Theo seemed to be using up his last ounce of energy to put Mrs Jessop and her companions off. 'But Claudia, Helen and I all have patients to see this morning, so we'll need to plan something another time.'

'Why don't you fill everyone in on your plans to raise awareness about the threat to the surgery, Stacie?' Claudia smiled at Mrs Jessop and the two other women. 'I'm sure you'll have lots of brilliant ideas and if we all work together on this, we might just pull it off. Just make sure you save me a bit of that wonderful coffee and walnut cake.'

'Will do, Doctor.' Mrs Jessop nodded sagely at Claudia, as though they were co-conspirators. Who'd have thought a few weeks before that Mrs Jessop would lead the charge to try and save the surgery?

★ ★ ★

Despite her bravado about stopping the sale of the surgery, Claudia felt as though a cloud was hanging over her as she worked through her list of patients. Forcing herself to ease the concerns of patients with no more than a cold was always difficult, but it was even trickier when there were very real things to worry about. Theo had made an error of judgement in not asking Stacie to keep the news about the surgery closure confidential. She might only have told Nicola initially, but the news seemed to have spread to everyone who came into Claudia's consulting room. After a while, repeating the mantra that there was nothing to worry about yet became very wearing, especially as she didn't really believe what she was saying. It seemed so unfair that she had finally found somewhere she wanted to call home and now it was being taken away from her; before she'd even had a chance to get used to the idea.

Mr Connor was one patient Claudia always had time for. He suffered with Multiple Sclerosis, but he had a constant smile on his face. Theo had said he always looked on the bright side, even when his MS was relapsing. Thankfully, on that Monday morning, he was still in the period of remission he'd been experiencing ever since Claudia had known him. Even the news about the possible closure of the surgery didn't seem to have dampened his good mood too much.

'How's my favourite doctor?' Mr Connor asked the question as he came into the consulting room.

'I'm okay, Jack. More to the point how are you?' Since he hadn't opened with a comment about the surgery closure, like almost every other patient she'd seen, Claudia decided not to mention it. Jack Connor had enough on his plate, without her trying to rope him in to the 'save the surgery' campaign.

'I'm doing great at the moment, thanks, Doctor Taylor.' Jack had a twinkle in his blue eyes that must have been dangerous when he'd been a younger man. It was surprising to see him without his wife, Debbie; they were usually inseparable and Claudia had never seen Jack on his own since she'd been at the surgery. 'I just came to see you to make sure I'm okay to travel.'

'I didn't realise you were off on holiday?' Claudia checked his notes on the screen, to check whether he and Debbie had been in to see Theo recently to discuss their plans, but there was nothing noted down.

'Debbie seems to think I'm made of

glass these days.' Jack gave her a wry smile. 'She won't book anything further afield than Cornwall, just in case something goes wrong.'

'It's perfectly possible to travel whilst you're in periods of remission like this. As long as you take a few basic precautions.' Claudia's words were met with a nod of approval from Jack.

'You and I know that, Doctor Taylor, but Debbie seems to think I'm the exception to the rule and that something awful will happened if we even leave the South West.' For once Jack looked a bit less cheerful. 'It doesn't matter how many websites I show her of MS suffers trekking through the Bornean Jungle, she still seems to think a cottage in St Ives is the biggest risk we can afford to take.'

'Just how adventurous is this holiday you've got planned then?' Claudia held her breath, waiting to hear whether Jack was planning some extreme sports, or the sort of long haul flight that really might take its toll on his health if things didn't go according to plan.

'Only Venice. We had our honeymoon there and I always promised I'd take her back one day. Only the two kids came along and then I got the MS diagnosis and it put our plans on hold. It's coming up to our twentieth anniversary now and both the kids are out and about, Annabel's at university and James is on a gap year in Australia, so it seems like the ideal time.'

'Well I can't see any major difficulties in that case, as long as you're still feeling well.' Claudia made a note on the computer. 'Obviously there are a few basic precautions you can take, like travelling with a letter from me explaining a bit about your condition, and it might be useful to have an Italian translation of it just in case. I always advise patients to keep their medication in the original packaging too, so the customs officers can see exactly what you are taking and why you need it.'

'Roger that.' Jack's cheerful demeanour had already been restored.

'The other thing to bear in mind is that flying and general tiredness can give you some pseudo-symptoms for a little while afterwards that can mimic the MS relapsing. They should disappear within twenty-four hours, though, otherwise they could be genuine symptoms making a return. Thankfully heat at this time of year in Venice shouldn't be an issue.'

'I thought that too. I just want to take Debbie for a meal in St. Mark's Square, like we did all those years ago, and thank her for all she's done for me since I've been ill and throughout our whole marriage really. She's always put me first and I just want to pay her back a bit, even if she'll be really cross with me when she first finds out.'

'Is it a surprise then?' Claudia smiled at the thought. Couples like Debbie and Jack were such a perfect contrast to her parents' relationship; that selfless love that meant putting the other person first at least half of the time, rather than one of them just bending the other to their will.

'It'll be a complete surprise, although *shock* might be a more accurate word. My daughter came home from university for the weekend and did all the bookings for me. She sorted out the insurance too and even let the airline know, so they can make arrangements to get us to the plane if I need any help.'

'It sounds like you have it all in hand then. I'll get Stacie to organise a letter for you and you should be able to pick that up from tomorrow onwards.' Claudia added a couple more details to Mr Connor's records. 'If Debbie has any major concerns, please tell her that she's welcome to give me a ring or to come in and see me.'

'I will do, Dr Taylor. We don't leave until next month, so I'll leave it a while yet to tell her.' Jack stood up to leave. 'We're going to make sure this surgery's saved you know. Mrs Jessop has already got me signed up to the committee she's setting up. We can't afford to let you and Dr Harrison go, you're the life blood of this place.'

'I think it's people like you and the community that make St. Finbar's Cross what it is, Jack. Everyone at the surgery really appreciates what it is you're doing for us, though.'

'Just one more thing, Doctor.' Jack hesitated as he got to the door.

'Of course, what is it?'

'Don't give up on the things you really want, will you? Even if we can't save the surgery, there are plenty of reasons for you to stick around. Not least Dr Harrison.'

'I'll bear that in mind.' Claudia looked up and couldn't help but return Jack's smile. It seemed the threatened closure of the surgery wasn't the only news travelling around St. Finbar's Cross like wildfire.

13

It was the following Saturday afternoon before the new elected committee of the 'Save the Surgery Fund' had arranged their first public meeting in the village hall. Mrs Jessop had been elected Chairwoman and Stacie was in charge of media relations and the marketing campaign. Claudia couldn't help but think they might have ruled the world in other circumstances; they were certainly a formidable combination.

The village hall had been set up with rows of orange chairs facing the stage, with a table at the centre, complete with Mrs Jessop wielding a wooden gavel which she'd apparently borrowed from the Parish Council. There was a general buzz of anticipation in the room by the time Claudia and Theo arrived, hand-in-hand. Any pretence that they weren't together had fallen by the wayside over the past week. The village seemed to have decided that they were made for each other, even before they were sure of it themselves. After surgery each day, they'd spoken at length about what might happen if the fundraising all came to nothing and they couldn't secure any finance from elsewhere in time, which unfortunately looked like an increasing possibility. The thought of leaving never once crossed Claudia's mind. Even if she didn't work there anymore, St. Finbar's Cross had become her home, not least because it was where the man she'd fallen in love with called home too.

Sean and Janey had joined them for dinner one evening, whilst Laura and Marcus were staying with his sister. As usual, Sean had made no bones about what he thought the next step in their relationship should be.

'So when am I going to get to be best man then? I've been practising so I can do wheelies going up the aisle.'

'Why do I know you're not joking?' Janey threw up her hands in mock despair, but the smile didn't once slip from her face.

'It's all a bit soon for that. It's been quite a whirlwind, my new life in St. Finbar's Cross.' Claudia spoke first, embarrassed that Theo had been put on the spot like that.

'Well I was just going to say that I'd marry Claudia tomorrow if she'd have me. But, in light of that, I think I'll let her take things at her pace.' Theo put his arm around her waist and pulled her closer to him. 'I'm just glad she wants to stay in St. Finbar's Cross, whatever else happens.'

'Cheers to that.' Sean raised his glass and the others followed suit. 'Only don't wait too long for that wedding, will you? If I learn many more tricks in this thing, I'll outshine you both.'

'I somehow doubt that.' Theo looked at Claudia as if she were the one person in the world who mattered most to him, something she'd never had before. 'Dr

Taylor is impossible to outshine.'

As difficult as she found it to take compliments, after a lifetime of being put down, those were words she knew she'd never forget.

★　★　★

The morning before the meeting in the village hall, Claudia and Theo had taken a walk up to the cross on the hill behind the surgery which gave the village its name. They'd gone inside the fenced off area and made their way to the centre of the cross, making the silent wishes that the legend of St. Finbar promised would come true. Part of Claudia felt guilty for asking for more, when she'd finally found a place she could call home, with wonderful new friends and a man who thought the world of her. But this wish wasn't about her, it was about all the people who had made her feel she belonged in St. Finbar's Cross — Theo, Stacie, Nicola, Danny, Jack Connor and, perhaps most of all, Mrs Jessop, whose turnaround had affected Claudia the most. This wish was for them.

⋆　⋆　⋆

By the time they got to the village hall, Claudia was feeling far less hopeful. It was an incredible amount of money to try and raise in a community as small as St. Finbar's Cross. Never mind wishes, it was going to take a minor miracle to pull this off.

'Right, everyone, order, order!' Mrs Jessop banged her gavel on the table in front of her, just as Claudia and Theo slipped into their seats. 'We all know what we're here for. We need to find a way of raising four hundred thousand pounds to save the surgery buildings in the village, so that we don't have to merge with the one in Bassington.' The way Mrs Jessop said it, it sounded like a fate worse than death.

'So far we've had donations in totalling almost two thousand pounds.'

Stacie smiled up at the audience and Claudia wondered how many of them were thinking the same thing as she was, that this was an amount of money they just couldn't hope to come up with from the community itself. The village had a lot of young families and retired people, who just didn't have huge sums of money to spare. And why should they? The prospect that no bank would take the risk of loaning them the money, and that the Trust didn't want to step in, filled Claudia was a growing sense of injustice.

'Thank you, Stacie. Now I think your mum, Nicola, is going to tell everyone why it's so important that we keep fighting to keep the surgery in the village?'

Nicola, who was a couple of rows in front of Claudia, stood up to address the crowded hall, visibly shaking at the prospect of speaking to so many people at once. 'As most of you know, my son Danny has Cystic Fibrosis. It means he spends a lot more time in hospital and at the doctor's than any boy of his age should have to do.' Her voice wobbled for a moment, the emotion of the situation clearly getting to her. 'Danny has got to know the doctors and the practice nurse at the surgery really well over the years. They know him too and he's not just another patient to them, he's *Danny*. They know how to put him at ease and when things are troubling him, even before he says anything. If we lose that sort of service, that sort of caring in our community, then we will have lost a very rare prize indeed. Please don't just stand by and let this happen. If we *all* help, if we *all* take part in the fundraising events, we can make this happen.'

Tears burned at the back of Claudia's eyes, as Nicola finished speaking to a thunder of applause and a standing ovation. If strength of emotion on its own was enough to pull the funds together, they'd be rolling in cash in no time at all. Sadly emotion didn't hold much sway with the bankers they really needed to convince, if they were going to raise the money in time.

'Thank you, Nicola, for that impassioned appeal. So what have we got planned so far?' Mrs Jessop addressed Jack Connor, who was sitting to her right, as the cheers from the audience finally quietened down. The door at the back of the hall opened letting in an icy blast. Claudia didn't turn around to see who the latecomers were, though; she couldn't seem to take her eyes off Mrs Jessop, who appeared to be relishing every moment of holding court.

'There's going to be a wine and wisdom evening next Friday and a bake sale on the fifteenth. Gregory Tallings is going to run the marathon, and use his sponsorship for the fund, and Hazel Jennings is going to organise a bring and buy sale at the beginning of next month.'

'Splendid.' Mrs Jessop banged her gavel again to bring the room back to attention, as chattering began to break out in individual rows. 'Has anyone else got anything they want to put forward, as a potential fundraising idea?'

Several arms shot up around the room and Mrs Jessop went to each person in turn.

'We're planning to hold a murder mystery evening at the Golden Fleece Hotel.' Mrs Smithson, Claudia's landlady, spoke up from the right hand side of the room. 'We've raised a couple of thousand pounds on nights like that before.'

'The children are going to have a wear what you like day and a sponsored car wash.' One of the teachers from the local primary school was next up to put forward the children's ideas.

'I thought I could hold a barn dance up at my farm.' Tom Higgins, a local dairy farmer, had a booming voice that could even compete with Mrs Jessop. Claudia could just imagine him calling out for the dancers to *take their partners by the hand*.

'This is all excellent stuff. We just need to make sure we coordinate on dates, so that it doesn't all happen at once.' Mrs Jessop glanced at Jack Connor as she spoke and he scribbled something down on the notepad in front of him. Never mind having to face up to his wife's wrath when he admitted booking the trip to Venice, becoming Mrs Jessop's personal assistant was probably even more of a challenge. 'Are there any other ideas before we move on to the next item on the agenda?'

Mrs Jessop seemed to scan the room and then pause. 'Yes, at the back with your hand up. What was it you wanted to add?'

'I'd like to make donation.' Claudia recognised the voice even before the person speaking stood up, so he could clearly be seen by everyone in the room. Her father didn't have a distinctive accent, but there was no mistaking him nonetheless.

'That's very generous of you, but we had planned to move on to donations later in the meeting.' Mrs Jessop waved a copy of the agenda at him. 'You should have one of these on your seat.'

'I know and I'm sorry to deviate from your plans, but the size of the donation — although it's really more of an investment — could make a difference to the rest of the things you're planning to discuss.' It seemed to Claudia as if every head in the room suddenly swivelled to look at her father.

'And exactly how much would you like to contribute?' Mrs Jessop's voice broke the tension.

'Four hundred thousand pounds.' Just four little words and for moment you could have heard a pin drop. Then it started, slowly at first, building to a thunderous cheer that Claudia wondered if they could hear back in Manchester. Who'd have believed it? Meek and down-trodden Geoffrey Taylor was the hero of the hour. Claudia only hoped it wasn't too good to be true.

*   *   *

'Dad, what on earth are you doing here?' Claudia fought her way through the crowd of people who were patting her father on the back and waiting to shake his hand.

'I came to see if I could help.' He said it as though all he'd offered to do was come and help her to change a flat tyre or something. 'I was Googling St. Finbar's Cross whilst we were at the boring conference your mother signed us up for. I really liked the look of the place when we visited and, until your mother dragged us down here to ruin things, you sounded as though it was making you really happy. When I entered the village name in the search engine, a load of stuff came up about the save the surgery fund and I just knew I had to help.'

'It's not that I'm not grateful, Dad, but we can't promise these people things that we aren't going to be able to deliver on.' Claudia frowned. 'In a million years Mum isn't going to allow you to invest money like that in a place like this, especially not in a GP's surgery of all things.'

'This money has got nothing to do with your mother.' Claudia had never seen her father look so determined. 'It's from the sale of Granny's house, which she instructed was to be split between you and me. Except your mother wanted to save the money for you in case she could persuade you to take up a specialist post in a hospital, or at least practise as a GP somewhere she deemed more exciting. I wanted to tell you about the money when we came down to the fete, but you know your mother. I take it you've got no objection to investing your half in the surgery? Because we'll need both shares of the money to make this work.'

'Of course not, but are you sure you want to use your half like that?' Claudia was numb with shock, aware that she should be elated but at the same time barely able to process it all.

'I've never been more certain of anything and, what's more, I've resigned from my consultancy at the hospital.' The smile on his face would have rivalled one of Jack Connor's. 'I'll have to work out my notice, of course, but I'm not quite ready to completely retire, so I was thinking of doing some locum-type work. I originally trained as a GP, after all, before your mother persuaded me to change direction. Maybe I could cover the surgery for you and Theo sometimes?'

'Oh Dad, I don't know what to say.' Claudia moved into his embrace; out of view of her mother, it felt completely relaxed for once. 'But what about Mum, what's she going to make of all of this?'

'I've told her my decision and it's her choice whether she wants to realign her priorities and start thinking a bit less about work and a bit more about us or not, but I've got to start living my own life whilst there's still time.'

'Mr Taylor.' Theo suddenly appeared beside them, having no doubt faced his own battle through the crowd. 'I'm delighted to meet you and thanks so much for stepping in to save the surgery.'

'My pleasure, but please call me Geoffrey. Or at the very least Dr Taylor, I'm dropping the Mr bit that came with being a consultant from here on out.' Geoffrey looked at Claudia. 'And is this the young man who persuaded you to stop trying to please your mother?'

'Theo made me realise that I should stop apologising for what I wanted to do with my life.' She was still struggling to make sense of what her father's decision could mean for them all, but she couldn't stop smiling.

'In that case, it's me who should be thanking you.' Geoffrey put a hand on Theo's shoulder.

'Claudia is the best thing that's ever happened to me, and to the whole village for a long time, and now the two of you have come up with a solution to save the surgery. I definitely think I'm the one who needs thank you. We pay our debts in St. Finbar's Cross, though, so if there's ever anything I can do for you . . .' Theo paused and another slow smile spread across her father's face.

'Just give my daughter the happiness she deserves.'

'You can count on that, Dr Taylor.'

Claudia looked from her father to Theo, realising she'd was home, surrounded by the people she loved most. St. Finbar's Cross had lived up to its reputation and granted every wish — even the ones she hadn't dared to make.

We do hope that you have enjoyed reading this large print book.

Did you know that all of our titles are available for purchase?

We publish a wide range of high quality large print books including:
Romances, Mysteries, Classics
General Fiction
Non Fiction and Westerns

Special interest titles available in large print are:
The Little Oxford Dictionary
Music Book, Song Book
Hymn Book, Service Book

Also available from us courtesy of Oxford University Press:
Young Readers' Dictionary
(large print edition)
Young Readers' Thesaurus
(large print edition)

For further information or a free brochure, please contact us at:
Ulverscroft Large Print Books Ltd.,
The Green, Bradgate Road, Anstey,
Leicester, LE7 7FU, England.
Tel: (00 44) **0116 236 4325**
Fax: (00 44) **0116 234 0205**

SUMMER LOVE

Jill Barry

1966: When Liz Lane arrives at Rainbows Holiday Camp in Devon to work as secretary to the entertainments manager, she is thrown into a world of sand, sun and fun, despite the long hours. Her boss suspects his new secretary will be a hit with the holidaymakers, and before long Liz is wearing a Rainbows uniform. But she ends up at loggerheads with Rob, the chief host, despite their mutual attraction to each other. Will love find a way?

FALLING FOR DR. RIGHT

Jo Bartlett

In the wake of her mother's death and a broken engagement, Dr. Evie Daniels decides to travel the world, doing everything her mum never had the chance to. Leaving her London job, she accepts a temporary locum position in the remote Scottish town of Balloch Pass, where she finds herself enjoying the work and community — and her handsome colleague Dr. Alasdair James. The feeling is mutual — but Alasdair is bound to Balloch Pass, whilst Evie is committed to spreading her wings . . .

THE ART OF LOVE

Anne Holman

Hazel Crick is furious when her entry for the Town Art Show is rejected. Convinced her colleague Jon Hunter is responsible, she accuses him of vetoing her painting out of spite. Later that day, she waits beside Jon's car to apologise. But this puts her in the wrong place at the wrong time: she is grabbed, bound, gagged, and bundled into Jon's car — unbeknownst to him. The two are about to be flung together in a hair-raising European adventure . . .

A GERMAN SUMMER

Carol MacLean

When her younger sister Stella disappears, it's up to Jo to find her and bring her home. It soon becomes clear that Stella has gone to Germany to stay with Jo's childhood penpal Max, with whom she has secretly been corresponding. As the sisters enjoy Max's hospitality in his splendid castle, Jo discovers that the grown-up man is very different to the boy she once knew — and very attractive, too. But staying in Germany is not an option, especially when her ill mother needs her back home . . .

LOVE'S LANGUAGE

Sarah Purdue

Sophie Carson has always dreamed of being a teacher, and now finally she has the chance. Due to start her training in Wales, there is only one problem: she must be able to read and write in Welsh. While studying, she works at the caravan site in Anglesey previously owned by her grandparents — and meets David, the heartbroken son of the new owners. Can Sophie convince him to help her with her studies, as she tries to help him mend his broken heart?